Angels Among Us
Life's Outtakes Year 7

52 Humorous And Inspirational Short Stories

By
Daris Howard

A collection of stories, humorous anecdotes, thoughts, and tidbits of wisdom from the popular newspaper column.

Publishing Inspiration

Angels Among Us

Life's Outtakes - Year 7

52 Humorous And Inspirational Short Stories

By

Daris W. Howard

A collection of stories, humorous anecdotes, thoughts, and tidbits of wisdom from the newspaper column **Life's Outtakes**.

ISBN-10: 162986000X
ISBN-13: 978-1629860008

www.publishinginspiration.com

Publishing Date: January 2014

Publishing Inspiration LLC

Table Of Contents

Dear Reader,

People often ask me if my stories are true. Though I must admit that I tend to take a bit of literary license in my writing, each story is based on an actual event. Sometimes the stranger stories are the ones that are stretched the least. As people often say, truth is stranger than fiction.

I also want to note that some of the names have been changed to protect the anonymity of the individuals.

Daris Howard

Value For Value

I watched as a man walked up to the donation table. "Would you like to donate?" the lady asked.

"Giving something for nothing ain't our way," the man replied. "We give value for value. But I did bring in some fudge that my wife made for the baked food table."

He plopped it in front of the lady who was tagging such things. He stayed there and watched as she put a price on it.

"Ten dollars?" he said, almost in disgust. "You ain't never tasted my wife's fudge, have you? Ten dollars don't even come close to how good it is."

"What price do you think we should put on it?" the woman at the table asked.

"I don't think you should sell that fudge for less than 25 dollars," he replied.

"But I'm not sure it will sell priced that high," the lady answered.

"Oh, it will sell," the man answered. "I can guarantee it."

The lady looked doubtful, but changed the price. "That's more like it," the man said. He then plopped down $30 on the table, and picked the fudge back up. "Keep the change," he said.

A man in our community had had a farming accident, and while he was in the hospital struggling to live, our community was having a fund raiser. It was spring, one of our busiest times of the year, but all work was set aside. Everyone was doing whatever they could to support the family and help them defray the hospital costs.

Everyone donated something. Women had brought hand tied quilts and lots of baked goods. I brought books. Others brought paintings. Farmers brought potatoes, gravy, beef, and all the fixings. A meal was five dollars, but, more than once, I watched as people plopped down a hundred dollar bill, and then left before change could be tendered.

When my family finished eating, I purchased a pie and some cookies, and then we joined others in the auditorium for the auction.

The auctioneer held up a painting, and began his singsong bidding. "How much will you give me for this painting? Who will give me a 50 dollar, dollar? Who will give me a 50?"

A hand went up, and the auctioneer pointed to the man. "I've got a 50. Who will give me a 60 dollar, dollar? Who will give me a 60?"

Another hand went up and the auctioneer pointed at the woman. "I've got a 60. Who will give me a 70 dollar, dollar? Who will give me a 70?"

The bidding continued with the man and the woman continuing to bid. "Hey, John," someone yelled. "Ain't that your wife you're a bidden' against?"

John and his wife turned and looked across the auditorium at each other, and sure enough, they were the two bidding. Amidst the laughter, John said, "Well, maybe she didn't think I was bidding enough for it, since she is the one who painted it."

John ended up winning the bid at $100. He paid the money and took the painting from the stage. He disappeared with it out of the back of the auditorium. A few minutes later I saw him, ever so carefully, trying to stay hidden, slip the painting back through the side stage door.

Soon the painting was brought to the front of the stage again. The auctioneer raised his hand. "We have a nice painting here. So who will give me a 50 dollar, dollar? Who will give me a . . . ?"

The auctioneer paused and looked deeply at the painting, then turned to John. "John, didn't you just buy this painting?"

John shrugged. "My wife is a prolific artist of one landscape."

He paid another $100 for it. And two times more he bought the same painting. I watched others buy something only to donate it back to be auctioned again.

Yes, sir. That's how it is in our farming community. We don't just donate; we expect equal value for things.

But the true value is never in the things that are sold, but in the hearts of these good people.

The Bad Hair Day

My little nine-year-old daughter, Elliana, came down the stairs to where I was making breakfast. "Dad, I need to dress up like in the olden days for school today."

"Okay," I answered. "We have some pioneer costumes in the closet downstairs. You can look through them."

"No," she replied. "Not the pioneer days. The 70's and 80's, when you were younger. What did you wear back then?"

It took me a minute to recover from hearing the years I went to high school called the olden days. When I finally did, I told her she probably ought to ask her mother for something that girls wore.

Elliana found her mother, and asked if we had something she could wear for 70's and 80's days at school.

"The olden days," I added.

"But I don't want to look stupid," Elli complained.

"We didn't look stupid," I told her.

One of my older daughters chimed in. "Have you looked at your yearbook lately?"

"Yes," I answered, "and we didn't look stupid." I paused for a moment, and then added, "Okay. Maybe bellbottoms were the exception."

My wife, Donna, found Elli a dress. It kind of just draped around her. I had forgotten that girls wore those unflattering dresses, but the dress didn't seem to bother Elli.

"Elli, you better come upstairs and let me do your hair," Donna said.

"How are you going to do it?" I asked. "The Farrah Fawcett feathered look?" That was the one thing I remembered about girls' hair from that era.

"What else was there back then?" she replied.

"I thought that was a very nice hairstyle," I said.

"That's because you didn't have to spend an hour doing it,

4

nor did you have to worry about a high forehead," Donna answered back.

The two of them went upstairs, and I finished making breakfast. It took them so long I was sure I would be late getting the kids to school, and me to work. When I finally told them they had to hurry, Donna called down that they were almost done.

She then hurried downstairs to help finish up the morning schedule. Meanwhile, Elli turned around and looked for the first time at herself in the mirror. Suddenly we heard a horrible scream. "Aww! I look horrible!"

She came down the stairs, her eyes full of tears. "Mom, what did you do to me?"

"Honey," her mother answered, "that is the way we always used to do our hair."

"But I look so stupid," she wailed.

"But that is the way your mother always used to look," I said.

Suddenly, everyone turned to look at me, and everything went quiet in the house except for Elli's sniffling. That was when I realized my choice of words and my timing left a lot to be desired. I decided it might be a good time to retreat out to the van.

Donna helped Elli brush out a portion of the feathering from her hair, and we finally were on our way. When we pulled in to her school, Elli paused before she got out. She just watched the other kids briefly, and then turned back to me. "I don't feel so bad now. Everyone looks stupid. And the boys look even stupider than the girls."

With that, she skipped off to class, feeling better, while I felt worse.

Later that day, when I picked her up, she was wearing her normal clothes that she had stuffed into her pack before school. Her hair was also brushed straight. When I asked her why she had decided to change, she shrugged.

"I couldn't stand to look stupid like that one minute longer than I had to," she replied.

Most of my college students are bright, fun to teach, and work hard. But each semester I get interesting letters, emails, and phone calls from a few students. I save these, and, occasionally, I compile them into a column. The last couple of years I have shared some of these, and, with school just starting, I thought I'd share a few more. I don't think any of these comments need any explanation, other than to say that I changed or removed any names for anonymity. Also, I pared down a few of them a bit.

Dear Professor Howard, This is Aaron from your 10:15 class. I guess you know from my grade that I have done worse and worse on each test until I am now failing your class. It just seems that the farther along we go, the more boring your class is, and the harder it is to concentrate. So, I was wondering what time you teach next semester so I can sign up for your class again.

Hello Professor Howard, I was just checking my grade online and it says I have an F. I'm not quite sure why that is. Could it be because I haven't turned in any of my projects and I bombed the test? Just checking.

Professor Howard, I'm sure you want to know why I am so far behind on my work in your class, so I thought I should tell you. I have been sick, and I can't do homework because reading your math stuff just makes me sicker.

Dear Professor Howard, I want you to know that I just checked my grades. I found out that I have missed a whole bunch of assignments that I forgot to turn in, and my grade is suffering. I want you to know that I am concerned about this because it doesn't reflect what I have been doing in the class. I just didn't realize a person had to turn in stuff to get credit for it.

Professor Howard, I want you to know that I took your multiple choice placement test. I feel like I almost knew every answer but I still got 0 on each of them. Somehow I feel I can do better than that.

Dear Professor Howard, I called and left a message about getting into your class and you never answered back. I was very upset, but then I realized that I never told you who I was or how to get hold of me, and my phone blocks showing its caller id. So I am including my information in this email this time, and hoping there is still room to add.

Dear Professor Howard, I am a student in your class and my name is Danyell. I just thought I should explain about the strange spelling of my name. It is actually pronounced just like Daniel, and, yes, I am a guy not a girl. The reason it is spelled strange is that when I was born, my mother wasn't feeling too well, so she passed the paperwork to my father to fill out, and he is a terrible speller.

Dear Professor Howard, I just wanted to write a thank you note. I want you to know that I really enjoyed your class this semester and I'm glad I took it. I didn't plan to because I saw that you are a writer, and I didn't think someone that is a writer could ever be a very good math teacher.

Professor Howard, I need to apologize. I wrote you an email telling you that I would miss class. I then realized that your class was Monday, Wednesday, and Friday, not Tuesday like I was thinking. So I actually made it to class. I'm sorry about making it to class when I told you I wouldn't.

Professor Howard, I am sorry I am going to miss class today. I came down with something dreadful and I have already spread it to my roommates and those who live close to me. They already hate me for it, so I thought it would be best to not spread it any further.

We brought our bikes to a stop at the top of the steepest hill in Binghamton, New York. I was breathing hard, but, Evans, the young man with whom I worked, was barely panting.

"You need to get in better shape," he commented.

I wanted to remind him of the reason I was more tired than he was. My bike weighed about as much as a small car, while his was light, sleek, and weighed about as much as a postage stamp.

In addition, I had about 70 pounds of books and other presentation material strapped to mine. Evans, afraid of scratching his new bike, refused to take anything on it besides himself.

But, before I could remind him how uneven things were, he headed down the hill.

The road down the hill was about two miles long. At the bottom it made a T. On the right was a huge mall; on the left were houses; and straight ahead was a large, open pasture with a barbed wire fence.

After Evans left, I paused for a few more breaths. Then I started on my way, too. He was about a quarter of a mile ahead of me, but, with all the added weight on my bike, and the steep downhill slope, my bike quickly picked up speed.

I knew the speed limit on this road was 45 miles per hour, and, as I sped past a car traveling the same direction, I grew concerned. I decided that it was more important for me to slow down than to catch up to Evans.

I applied the brakes carefully, and a smell of burning rubber filled the air. The steepness of the incline and the extra weight continued to propel me forward with an inertia the brakes couldn't handle. I applied more and more pressure, but my speed increased, even as my bike began to vibrate violently, threatening to throw me into the path of the cars.

But I had an even bigger problem. I was rapidly approaching

the intersection. If the light changed and I slid into oncoming traffic, my chance of survival would be in the single digits. I knew I had to make it through the light.

Evans, now less than 25 yards ahead of me, entered the intersection just as the light turned yellow. I released my brakes slightly, and I reached the intersection just as the light turned red.

At the speed I was going, I had to lean almost parallel with the pavement as I turned. But the amount of weight on my bike caused both tires to start sliding perpendicular to the direction my bike was aimed. When they hit the gravel on the side of the road, I could no longer hold it. I flipped, slamming into the gravel as my bike tumbled away. It hit the four strands of barb wire, snapping them.

I, too, tumbled through the new hole in the fence, grateful my bike had split the wires so I wouldn't be cut to ribbons. I bounced over and over, finally coming to rest in the pasture. People and cows came running from all directions.

A man knelt by me. "Are you all right?"

My pants were ripped off nearly to my waist, and patches of skin were torn off of my legs and my arms. The wounds were full of dirt and gravel, stopping the bleeding. I stood and nodded.

Everyone helped me gather my books and presentation materials. The last man to leave said, "That has got to be the worst bike crash I have ever seen. You shouldn't carry so much. It's a miracle you're alive."

My tank of a bike survived with only slightly bent tires, and after closing the fence the best I could, I climbed on my bike and wobbled away. I met Evans about a quarter of a mile down the road, where he had stopped and waited.

"Thanks for coming back to help," I said sarcastically.

"Hey," he replied. "I was embarrassed to have anyone know I knew you."

Then, after a short pause, he added, "Man, you really need to learn how to ride a bike better."

How Much Is A Bike Worth

I threw down my wrench in frustration, and went to find a better one. I was living in New York, working with a young man named Martin, and our only means of transportation were bicycles. Unfortunately I spent all of my free time fixing mine. I was only gone for about 15 minutes, but when I came back, my bike had been stolen. I couldn't believe it had disappeared so quickly.

I filed a police report, and did everything I could, but I knew the chance of recovering my bike was very small. I was disheartened about losing it. The money to buy it had been a gift from my grandfather. He had sent it after I wrecked my previous bike when I crashed through a barbed wire fence.

This time I had no gift money, and I didn't want to ask for any. So, while I searched for a cheap, used bike, Martin and I were reduced to walking. One day, while we were out working, we saw a man go by with three bikes. He was riding one, pulling one, and he had another one draped around his shoulders.

Martin nudged me. "Maybe we ought to follow him and see if he has seen yours."

An hour or so later, a young boy approached us, glancing nervously around as he spoke.

"Hey, Mistas. I sees yous twos a walkin'. I'se a thinkin' dat maybe you could use a bike. Well, my brudder needs some money real bad. 'Ees got a bike dat is good as new dat he'd sell real cheap. I'se a wonderin' if you's mawt be interested."

Martin smiled. "Yeah, we are kind of sick of walking."

"What kind of bike is it?" I asked.

The little boy glanced around more nervously. "What kin'a bike you want?"

Martin's smile turned to a grin. We, of course, knew why those bikes were so cheap. I patted the boy on the head. "I'm afraid we probably wouldn't be interested."

As the boy went away, Martin turned to me. "You know, you should have taken him up on it. Maybe we would have ended up finding your bike."

"Or, more likely," I answered, "I would have ended up with somebody else's stolen bike."

A few days later we were visiting with some of the other young men we worked with, and Martin told of our experience.

"You really should have gone with the boy," Taylor said.

"Nah," I answered. "I'm afraid there's a chance I could have seen my own bike, and I might have gotten angry. That wouldn't have been a good situation. It would be better for me to just find another cheap, legitimate bike somewhere."

"I had my bike stolen not too long ago, too," Taylor said, "and I think if you get a chance to buy your own bike back, you should. And you shouldn't feel bad about paying for it as long as you can dicker them down to a decent price."

I was shocked. "Are you kidding? Buy my own bike back? That's just senseless."

"I had thought so, too," Taylor replied. "But I originally bought my bike for more than $200, and I swear it was always breaking down. I wasted almost all of my free time trying to keep it running, when I would have rather spent that time writing letters home."

"What has that got to do with buying it back?" I asked.

"Well, after it got stolen, I found it at this place that was selling bikes. They had oiled it up, and totally repaired it. I ended up buying it back for only $10, and it has worked great ever since."

His grin widened as he continued. "I couldn't have gotten it fixed that well at a repair shop for ten times that amount. If they were smart, they would realize they could make more money as a bike repair shop than they do selling stolen bikes."

I smiled at that, and decided that if I ever did find my bike again, I might just pay the repair bill and buy it back.

A Super Ugly Bike

Since I had had my bike stolen, and didn't have a lot of money to buy another one, I was reduced to hunting for a used one. Friends of mine tried to help scare one up, talking to everyone they knew. Finally, one day, a lady called me.

"I understand you are looking for a cheap bike." When I told her I was, she continued. "I do believe I have an old one out in my shed. I would give you a really good deal on it."

My associate, Martin, made the nearly two mile trek over to her house with me. When we arrived, the lady led us out to her old shed. We helped her move piles of mostly useless junk that were stacked to the ceiling. We finally found the bike deep in the farthest corner.

Dragging it out into the light, I was stunned. It was probably the ugliest thing I had ever seen in my life. It was a girl's three speed, and was a relic from the 60's. It looked like it had been painted by someone who was high on something. Add to that the grime that embellished it, and it was absolutely ghastly.

"How much do you want for it?" I asked.

The lady looked at me, as if sizing up how much of a sucker I was. "Six bucks," she replied.

"Let me see how it runs," I said.

I turned it over and turned the crank. The wheel started to roll faster and faster. I tried to switch gears, but the cable was stuck, frozen solid with rust. It was locked in third gear, but it worked, and it worked well.

"I'll take it," I said.

Martin looked at me as if I had lost my mind. I dug into my pocket and pulled out what dollar bills I had, and then I counted change in dimes and quarters until I had enough.

As we walked away, with me dragging the bike, Martin rolled his eyes. "I have only one request."

"What's that?" I asked.

"That bike is so ugly I want you to always ride a hundred yards apart from me so no one knows I know you."

"It's not that bad," I said.

"It **is** that bad," Martin retorted.

He suggested we stop by the store and get me a bike lock. "A bike lock?" I scoffed. "Are you crazy? A lock costs $10, and the bike only cost $6."

"Well, when you get your bike stolen, you can only blame yourself," he said.

Once I got my bike home, I took some WD40 and sprayed it on all of the moving parts. I tested the bike and it rolled smoothly, though it was hard to start out in third gear. I took a rag and cleaned off the old dust and grime it had picked up from the shed, and the 60's paint job showed even more.

"You should have left the grime on it," Martin commented. "It actually looked better that way."

That evening we went to the hospital to visit a friend. I just flopped my bike against the fence, and then I waited for Martin, who spent 15 minutes locking his to a solid post. When he finished, Martin grinned smugly at me. "At least one of us will still have a bike when we come out."

We went in, had our visit, and when we came out, we had a surprise. Martin's bike was stripped to the frame. The pedals, the racks, the handle bars, and everything that wasn't secured by the bike lock was gone.

Next to Martin's bike skeleton sat my bike, still against the fence, still where I left it, still totally untouched. Martin stood there in shock.

"You were right," I teased. "One bike is still here."

Martin nearly choked. "I can't believe it. I never thought there could be a bike that was so ugly that the thieves wouldn't even want it, but I guess there finally is."

And, thus, I had solved my bike theft problem.

How Not To Name A Baby

Kevin hung around my desk after class was over, and I could tell he wanted to visit. When I turned to him to see if he had any questions, he said he would like to talk privately. Usually, this means a student is concerned about their grade, but he was a good student, so I was sure it must be something else.

As soon as I had gathered up my papers, we walked together to my office. Once there, he sat down, seeming nervous about what he had to say. I just waited, and finally he spoke.

"Professor Howard, I know you have a big family, and I am hoping you can give me some advice."

I was only slightly surprised by his statement, because I have had students ask for personal advice before. I told him I would do what I could.

"I think I told you that my wife and I are expecting our first baby," he said. "Well, we are having a problem."

"Is she having some complications?" I asked.

"Oh, no," he replied. "Nothing like that. It's just that she wants to name the baby Katy, and I can't stand that name. I have tried and tried to tell her. I hinted at first. Then I brought it up in casual conversation. Finally, I told her outright that I didn't want to name the baby that. She is still insistent that will be her name. This disagreement is really starting to strain our marriage."

"What can I do to help?" I asked.

"I was hoping you might have an idea how I can get her to change her mind."

I laughed. "There's one thing that I can just about guarantee will get her to change the name."

He leaned close. "What?"

"Tell her you have changed your mind and decided you like the name Katy because you had a former girlfriend with the same name. That will make her change it." I laughed again as I finished.

"I'm teasing of course."

I could tell by the look on his face that his mind was whirring as he spoke. "No, no. I really think it will work."

"But I was teasing," I insisted.

He was undeterred, and spoke as if deep in thought. "And you know what? I just thought of something else. There was a really pretty girl I liked when I was in junior high, and her name was Katy. But she wouldn't even give me the time of day." He then turned back to me. "Do you think that might be why I don't like the name?"

I shrugged. "Seriously, I'm not much of a psychologist."

He didn't care. He was already heading out the door. As he left, he said, "I think you just might have saved our marriage."

A few days later, Kevin joined me in my office again. He flopped in the chair. "Women are so strange."

"How so?" I asked.

"After I left here, I thought more and more about it, and I decided that Katy would be an okay name. But when I told my wife, she got suspicious and wanted to know why I had changed my mind. When I told her I knew a really pretty girl named that, she immediately changed the baby's name before I could even explain that the girl didn't like me. She then told me she decided we would name the baby Suzanne."

"What did you say to that?" I asked.

"I told her I was okay with it," Kevin replied, "and I am."

"I'm glad it worked out so you both found a name you like," I said.

"Yeah," he answered. "But I think it would be better if I don't tell her that I dated a girl named Suzanne when I was in high school."

Puppy Baseball

We have a new puppy that is only about four months old. She is a black Lab/Newfoundland cross, so she is already very good sized. Sasha has boundless energy, and she wants to be involved in everything.

That was why, when my two little girls decided that they wanted to play baseball together in the back yard, she was ready to join them. She doesn't know anything about baseball, or the rules of the game, but she does know that they had a tennis ball and a thing that looked like a stick, and those are two of her favorite toys.

Sasha watched curiously as my two daughters marked the play area and laid out the bases. Heather was first up to bat, so, when everything was set, she took up her position. Elli moved over to the pitching spot. She threw the ball, and Heather swung and missed. Immediately, Sasha, who had already learned about fetching, was there to retrieve it. She picked it up and trotted back to Elli with the ball in her mouth.

"Thank you, girl," Elli said, reaching for the ball.

Sasha has learned to fetch, but she hasn't learned to give up what she fetches. A slight tug-of-war ensued until Elli pulled the ball from Sasha's mouth. When she finally did get the ball, her grin turned to a grimace.

"Ooh, yuck!" Elli said. "The ball is all covered with dog slobber. Don't blame me if I throw a spit ball."

After shaking off what drool she could, Elli tossed the ball once more, and once more Heather missed. Immediately, Sasha was there to retrieve it. When Elli complained again about the ball, Heather said, "At least we don't need a catcher."

On the next toss, Heather hit the ball in a nice arc across the yard. Sasha took off after it. She retrieved it and headed back at full speed toward the girls. Seeing Heather running, Sasha seemed to assume she was coming after the ball, so she headed for Heather, still carrying the ball in her mouth.

Heather saw Sasha coming at her as she ran toward the base, and started yelling, "No, Sasha! No!" But the more she yelled, the more Sasha thought that she was running to get the ball. Sasha caught up to Heather and ran right into her path, causing Heather to tumble over her.

"Tagged out," Elli declared. Heather didn't feel that was correct call.

In their normal game, with only two of them, if they could get to one of the bases, they got to go back and bat again. Heather finally agreed to the out, and Elli moved to take a turn at bat.

Heather tossed the ball a couple of times before Elli hit it, while Sasha played catcher and retriever. Heather received no empathy from Elli for the slobbery ball.

When Elli hit the ball, it was almost directly back to Heather. Heather picked it up before Sasha could, and both girls raced for first base. Sasha wasn't sure what they were doing, but she decided that first base was place to go, so she joined in the chase.

Sasha arrived just ahead of the girls, and thinking the base was the object they were after, she picked it up and took off with it. Unable to touch the base, Elli chased after her, yelling at her to drop it. A game of tag ensued, in which Heather eventually caught up to Elli and tagged her out with the ball.

"That's no fair," Elli complained. "Sasha moved the base."

They played for quite a while, with Sasha changing the rules for them as they went. When I arrived home, they came running in to greet me, and to tell me about their game.

"So, who won?" I asked my two tired girls.

Their mother, who had watched the game through the window, was the one to answer.

"Sasha did, by a nose."

A Halloween Vendetta

As I was heading home from church on the Sunday before Halloween, Lenny grabbed me. "Hey, would you like to join Butch, Buster, and me on Halloween?"

"Is this about getting your uncle again?" I asked.

I had heard of Lenny's vendetta to get the best of his uncle each year on Halloween, and how each time it ended up with his uncle getting the best of him and whoever went with him.

"Yes," Lenny said, "but this time I have the perfect idea to make sure we get him good."

He looked around to make sure no one else was listening to us, and then carefully pulled out a piece of paper bearing a carefully detailed plan.

"This year we will have our sweet revenge," Lenny said with a grin.

"Isn't that what you said last year?" I asked.

"Yeah," Lenny replied. "But last year's plan was too complex. This year it will be quick and simple, and, with my forethought and preparation, we won't be wandering through his mucky corral again."

I knew I wouldn't be able to join them. I had chores I had to do that would take me most of the evening, and then I would have to be back up early the next morning to do them again before school. My dad always said that the best way to keep a boy out of trouble was to have plenty of work for him to do, and, with 120 head of milking cows, I had plenty to do. How I despised those cows!

I told Lenny I would have to decline.

"Too bad," he said, as he headed on his way. "You'll miss all the fun."

Halloween night came, and Lenny, Butch, and Buster made their way under cover of darkness to Lenny's Uncle's farm. They parked a short distance down the road and sneaked quietly into the farm yard. Their goal was the old barn. Lenny knew that his uncle had a barrel of tarry molasses near the barn. They planned to rig a trip string that would tip the barrel, engulfing any unsuspecting victim in a wave of stickiness.

They worked their way stealthily across the yard, carrying some heavy duty fish line and some blocks. Everything worked according to plan. They moved the barrel into position along the path through the yard. Lenny strung the fish line between a shed and the barrel. Butch and Buster tilted the barrel, and Lenny put some blocks under the edge so it tilted at an angle such that the slightest movement would pull it over. Lenny pulled the fish line tight and tied it to the barrel.

"That should do it," Lenny said. "We'll get him for sure this year."

They all laughed quietly, and then Lenny led the way back across the yard. Just as they were about to pass the house, an outside light kicked on. Lenny froze, as did the others behind him. Suddenly, a figured jumped out of the house, dressed like an escaped demon, screeching a terrifying scream.

Lenny turned and crashed into Butch and Buster, who were scared so stiff they couldn't even run. Lenny knocked them down, bringing life to their frozen limbs. They scrambled all over each other, and finally made it to their feet.

They ran fast and blindly in the dark, with Lenny in the lead. Lenny remembered the trip wire just in time and stopped, only to have Butch and Buster plow into him.

Back in church the next Sunday, I was surprised, or maybe not, to see Lenny, Butch, and Buster all come in with their heads shaved bald.

"What happened to the three of you?" I asked.

"Lenny and Halloween is what happened to us," Butch grumbled. "Molasses doesn't come out of hair."

"Oh, quit your whining," Lenny snapped. "Your hair will grow back."

And that was one of the few times I was glad my dad had 120 cows for me to milk.

Football And Nylons

My daughter complained about her nylons twisting.

"I feel sorry for you having to wear those things." I said.

She rolled her eyes. "Dad, you don't know the half of it."

I smiled. I remembered back to the final high school football game of the regular season. As we ended practice, Coach called us together for a team meeting.

"Men, we are in for a tough game tomorrow. Adding to the challenge, the weather report predicts snow. I want you to dress warmly. You will want to wear a pair of your mother's nylons. Just make sure it is one of her older pairs and not a new one. We don't need any mothers mad at us again."

I laughed, thinking he was teasing us about wearing nylons, but no one else even smiled. When coach finished, we went to the locker room. I asked some of the other guys if Coach was serious about the nylons.

Lenny was first to reply. "Of course he was. Nylons help keep the moisture away from your skin so you don't freeze as much when all of your football gear gets wet. And he was serious about asking your mother for an older pair, too. Last time I took a pair of my mom's new ones, and Coach got an earful."

"Why?" I asked.

"Because they were too baggy and torn for her to wear after that."

I watched the others for signs that Lenny was trying to pull a fast one on me, but no one seemed the least bit interested in our conversation.

I still didn't trust him. I could remember Lenny talking Sam into wearing a supporter over his head for a nose warmer at the previous year's first track meet, claiming it would enhance his performance. I was sure he was taking advantage of my inexperience. However, I decided I would bring a pair and watch to see what everyone else did.

I considered every way I could think of to ask my mom for a pair, without sounding stupid. I considered going without, but the thought of being soaked by wet clothes didn't thrill me. Finally, I just came out and asked her if she had an old pair of nylons that I could have.

"What do you need them for?" she asked.

"Oh, just something at school," I replied.

She found an old pair that had a run in them. I told her I was sure it would work, though I really had no idea what I was doing.

Once at school, I made sure to keep them hidden. I decided to wait to pull them out until I made sure everyone else was really wearing some, too.

It finally came time to get ready for the game. I watched as Lenny whipped out a pair of nylons and started to wriggle his way into them. Lenny's mom was small and slender. Lenny was about the size of a small, fat truck. Seeing the nylons stretch around him helped me see why his mom would have been mad when he used her new pair.

As others began putting some on, I took mine out of my locker, and self consciously started the process. The hair on my legs rolled and pinched as I tugged and pulled, and, when they were finally in place, they made my legs itch. It made me grateful I wasn't a girl, having to wear them all of the time.

When Lenny turned to look at me, he said exactly what I was thinking about him. "Howard, you look like an absolute idiot."

"After all of this we better win this game," I grumbled back.

My daughter's words brought me back to present. "Dad, you men should have to wear some just so you know what it's like.

I smiled. "Yeah, I guess we should."

Football, Ice, And Snow

As we approached the last football game of the season - the final one that would determine if we made it to the playoffs - Coach reminded us that, above all, good sportsmanship was of highest priority. He also informed us that snow was predicted and told us to prepare for it.

"The worst part about snow," Lenny said, as we went to the locker room, "is, if it gets icy, then you slip and slide."

Keith jumped into the conversation. "What is this 'you' stuff? You big and clumsy linemen might slip and slide, but I won't."

Lenny just rolled his eyes. "Yeah, right."

That night, instead of snow, a slushy rain fell. Early the next morning the temperature dropped and the slush turned to ice. Just before the game, there was a light snow. Snow on ice makes it treacherous. It was almost impossible to stand, let alone walk or run, especially with cleats that acted like ball bearings on ice.

As we warmed up, we were slipping, sliding, and falling down. At least, everyone was except for Keith. He wasn't slipping at all. He mocked the rest of us for being clumsy oafs. But his stability didn't go unnoticed by Coach.

He called us all over. "Keith, let me see your shoes."

We watched as Keith reluctantly sat on the bench and held them up.

"That's what I thought," Coach said.

Keith had fancy shoes with cleats that could be changed out and new ones put in. He had screwed in spiked track cleats, which are against football rules, since they can rip into exposed skin.

Coach was not happy with him. "Win or lose, we don't break rules! Get the right ones in your shoes, or you will warm the bench!"

Embarrassed about being found out, Keith switched his

cleats. When he joined us on the field, he slipped and fell as much as anyone. When it was time for the game to start, we lost the toss and were to receive first. Our player caught the ball and was immediately tackled, as the other team hardly seemed fazed by the ice.

We couldn't make any yardage and soon had to punt. The other team worked their way to a touchdown, as we continued to slide and fall and they didn't. The reason for the difference became quite obvious when the cleats from one of the other team members left a huge, bloody gash the length of my arm. They had spiked cleats.

A timeout was called by the ref to bandage my arm, and he asked the young man for a look at his shoes. Reluctantly, the other player complied, and, when the ref saw the spikes, the young man was ejected from the game. The opposing coach yelled at the boy, saying he had told him not to wear them, but we were sure it was more of a show for the ref than reality. We were positive their whole team was wearing spikes, and it seemed impossible the coach wouldn't know.

While my arm was being bandaged, we complained to Coach about the disadvantage we faced. Coach told us he would prefer we lost than to have us break rules. We would just have to play as smart as we could. We did make one touchdown. On a guard trap play, I pulled and took out two defenders when I slipped and crashed into them. It opened up a clear path for Keith to make a run the length of the field, sliding safely into the end zone.

Though we were playing a superior game in many ways, the disadvantage had us down 21 to 7 at half time. As we took to the field for the second half, we were discouraged. But, as we kicked to them, the sky started dumping snow. Within minutes a good four inches covered the ice and packed quickly. Suddenly our cleats started finding traction.

With a determination intensified by the events of the first half, we played almost flawlessly. When the final buzzer sounded, the scoreboard showed us ahead 42 to 21. But more than the win, I will always remember what Coach said when we gathered for the team meeting.

"It's not the win I'm proud of you for, but the fact that you played with good sportsmanship against an overwhelming disadvantage. Good sportsmanship, after all, is truly the highest prize."

The Fall Camping Trip

When my sons, ages eight and ten, learned that I was taking my scouts on a fall campout, they begged to come with me. I was leery of taking them at that time of year. The weather could be unpredictable. There could be a forty degree temperature drop in just a few hours. If we ended up with freezing temperatures, it would be all I could do to take care of my scouts without having the responsibility of two small boys.

They continued to plead with me, so, the night before the camping trip, I turned on the news to check the weather report. The weatherman said the air was circulating from the south and would stay mild. With that reassurance, I told them they could go.

When I arrived home from work on the night of the campout, they were waiting. I hurried and changed into my camping gear. I made sure we all had long johns, heavy sweaters, thick coats, and warm, dry boots.

"But, Dad," the oldest complained, "we'll be too hot."

"You can always put on only what layers you need," I told him, "but you can't add on what you don't have."

We met at the church and loaded the scouts and gear into my van and into my assistant scoutmaster's truck. Soon, we were on our way.

When we arrived at the campsite, the evening was quite pleasant as we set up camp. I helped the boys that were supposed to cook dinner to get the fire going, and we started cooking. The other scouts headed off to play a game of steal the flag. I gave my sons some cookies I had brought to keep them satisfied until dinner was ready.

As we busily worked on the food, my assistant scout master came and put his hand on my shoulder. He pointed to the western sky. I turned to look at the black clouds that were rolling quickly toward us even us as he spoke. "I think we better hurry."

We called all of the boys in and had them recheck tent stakes as well as help move the dinner forward as fast as possible. The food was only about half done when the storm hit us. Wind blew everything everywhere. The fire would flame high, and then flicker almost to embers before rising high again. It made it almost impossible to keep an even heat.

Suddenly, a freezing sleet started to fall, and, with it, the temperature began to plummet. The scouts rushed to their tents. I hurried my sons into ours, got them into dry clothes and tucked into sleeping bags. Then I grabbed my rain coat and returned to finish cooking the food as best I could. While I did, the sleet worked its way through my rain coat in little freezing streams down my back.

By the time I finished cooking, all of the scouts had changed into dry clothes and bundled up in their sleeping bags, so my assistant and I took food around to them. After everyone else was fed, my assistant took some food and retired to his tent, while I took what was left to my tent to share with my sons.

It was the bottom of the pan, and was burnt from my struggles trying to keep a fire going in the freezing sleet. I fed my sons the best of it and choked down as much of the charcoaled remains as I could stand. I put on some dry clothes, and slid, shivering, into my sleeping bag for a long, sleepless night, wondering if I would ever get warm. As I did, my oldest son turned to me.

"Dad, what do you think Mom and the girls are doing right now?"

I thought of them, warm and comfortable at home. "They are probably eating pizza and watching a movie," I replied.

He sighed. "Poor girls. They never get to do anything fun like we do."

It was my second Thanksgiving far from home. I was invited to dinner by a family that I dearly loved. Norma, the mother, was a wonderful lady. Though she was blind, nothing slowed her down. She ran her home with efficiency and precision.

But there was something else that made her more amazing. She had eight children; four had mental disabilities, and the other four had physical disabilities. Each mentally challenged child was paired with a physically challenged child. Together they became a team. The mentally capable children would direct their physically able sibling. Together they could accomplish things neither could do alone.

When I asked Norma about her family, she told me her story. When they were young, she and her husband, Tom, had fallen in love and had married. They both loved children and couldn't wait for their first baby to come along. But, just about that time, both Norma and Tom contracted a terrible disease.

It was a disease that very often took a person's life. Though Norma and Tom both survived, each lost their sight. As devastating as that was, the fact that they would no longer be able to have children was even more disappointing to them.

After they learned to deal with their loss of sight, they decided that it was time to try to adopt some children. But every agency that they approached about adoption felt that it would be impossible for two blind parents to raise a child, and they were always turned down.

Finally, they applied to be foster parents. At first, the state would not place any children in their home. But, one day, Norma received a call. There was a young child that had a disability, and the state couldn't get anyone else to take her. Norma jumped at the chance. Though the state only meant it to be temporary, Norma and Tom showed they were very capable and, in fact, their own disabilities gave them more understanding and patience. It wasn't too long before the state allowed them to adopt Tina.

One after another, each time the state had a child that no one else wanted, Norma and Tom would take the child into their home, love them, and eventually receive permission to adopt them. And, thus, their family grew.

Then, due to complications from the disease, Tom's health started to fail. His passing was a great loss to the family, and the state was concerned whether Norma would be able to handle all of the children on her own. She informed them that her children were more important to her than anything else in her life, and she would be fine. As the state monitored the situation, they agreed, and, in fact, even allowed her to adopt one more child to round out her family.

Little Emily was the last, and was only six years old when she came into this unique family. She was a Down Syndrome girl. In her young life, she had been in home after home, some for less than a month, and none for more than a couple. By Thanksgiving she had been in Norma's home for almost a year, and, for the first time in her life, she had found consistency and security.

As the final touches for dinner were being finished, Norma invited me to read some stories to the children. Little Emily climbed on my lap, and all of the other children gathered around. I read some Bible stories appropriate for the season, as I felt that in this home there was a spirit truly representative of that day.

When we gathered around the table, as was their tradition, each person shared what he or she was most grateful for. When it was Emily's turn, she turned to look at Norma, and she smiled a smile Norma couldn't even see, speaking words I will never forget.

"I'm grateful for a momma that loves me."

Tears poured down Norma's face. It doesn't take seeing eyes to know love.

Our high school chemistry teacher flipped the fan switch in the chemistry lab, and a loud pop sounded. "Oh, shoot!" he exclaimed. "We can't do the experiment without the fan."

"Hey," Brent said. "My dad is an electrician, and I can wire almost anything. Do you want me to take a look at it?"

Mr. Hatsker shook his head. "Probably not, Brent. I'll acquisition the school to get it fixed."

"Are you sure?" Brent said. "I'm sure I could have it fixed in minutes."

"I better not," Mr. Hatsker said. "I probably need to go through the right channels."

"What about the due date on our lab project?" Marcy asked. "There is no way we can have it done by Friday."

"I will move that back a few days," Mr. Hatsker replied

Mr. Hatsker called the principal to come down, and they discussed the situation.

"Well, we can definitely have the district repairman come look at it," the principal said. "But I can't guarantee any time table on it. They are doing some remodeling at the district office."

"My lab should come first," Mr. Hatsker replied. "The problems with the lab have already put me a couple of weeks behind this semester."

The principal shrugged. "I will do my best."

Mr. Hatsker started us working on some new material in the book. We hadn't been at it very long when the principal came back. "I hate to tell you this, but they can't do it for a couple of weeks."

"A couple of weeks!" Mr. Hatsker exclaimed. "We can't wait a couple of weeks. We need it now."

The bell rang, and we gathered our books to leave. Brent hung around behind as the rest of us headed to lunch. As lunch was coming to and end, he joined us to quickly wolf down some food.

"Where have you been?" I asked.

He leaned over and whispered. "I fixed the fan in the chemistry room."

"I don't know if I am happy about that or not," I told him. "Now we'll have to do our lab projects."

"Beats studying from the book all class period," he replied.

The next day, Mr. Hatsker started to lecture.

"Aren't we going to go to the lab?" Brent asked.

"There's nothing we can do until the fan is fixed," Mr. Hatsker replied.

"But I think it is," Brent said.

Mr. Hatsker looked at him suspiciously, but we all traipsed into the lab to check it out. He flipped the switch, and, sure enough, the fan spun, rattled, and came to life. Mr. Hatsker shrugged and told us to all get busy. We pulled out the sulphuric acid at our stations and started to work. Soon, those of us closest to the fan started to cough and choke, and before long, everyone was.

"The fan is blowing backward!" Mr. Hatsker yelled. "Everyone, outside!"

He pulled the fire alarm as we headed out the door. I was the last student out, and I could hear screaming coming through a door in the chemistry lab that always remained locked. I had always thought it was a closet. Through my choking, I asked Mr. Hatsker where it led.

"It is a second entrance to the darkroom used by the year book class to develop pictures," he answered through his own coughing.

Within minutes, students were pouring out of every door, happy to be out of school. When they found it was because Brent wired the fan backward, they were high-fiving him.

But there was one person who wasn't happy. The yearbook advisor, coughing and choking, was marching determinedly in the direction of our celebrating, and she wasn't smiling. Brent saw her coming and tried to calm everyone's exuberance.

"Just act normal and remember, you don't know anything about any fan. We can just say it's a fire drill."

Just then a fire truck rushed up. Firemen jumped off, donned gas masks, and rushed into the building.

"A very realistic fire drill," Brent added.

Trying to fix the fan in the chemistry lab, Brent ended up wiring it backward, blowing the acidic gas back into our lab, as well as the rest of the school.

There was one group that was affected by it almost as much as we were. Unknown to most of us, the door in the chemistry lab that always remained locked was an emergency exit from the dark room that the yearbook class used. The trapped gasses from our lab flowed heavily into that room, as well.

Thus, when the fumes from our experiments drove us from the building, the yearbook class was also forced to exit at the same time. Our teacher, Mr. Hatsker, pulled the fire alarm on his way out, and soon the whole building was evacuated.

Getting out of class, even for a brief time, was cause for celebration. At least, it was until we saw Mrs. Kay, the yearbook advisor, marching doggedly in our direction, coughing and choking as she came, with her whole class right on her heels. She grabbed Mr. Hatsker by his shirt, and, even though she was shorter than he was, she nearly picked him off of the ground. "What in blazes name do you think you are doing in that fool chemistry lab of yours?"

"We were just doing an experiment," Mr. Hatsker replied through his own coughing.

"Experiment! What kind of experiment were you doing that would entail gassing everyone in the whole school?"

"Hey, it's not our fault," Mr. Hatsker replied. "The fan in the lab ran backward and blew the gasses back into the room. It wasn't pleasant for us either."

Mrs. Kay wasn't feeling any mercy and still didn't let him go. She stood up on her tip toes to bring herself nose to nose with him. "And how come you couldn't figure that out before you started the experiment and tried to kill everyone?"

Mr. Hatsker's own determination seemed to return, and he

jerked her hands from his shirt. "Don't go pushing me around. Didn't you get a whole lot of new equipment for your dark room this year, while my chemistry lab didn't get any funding at all? Maybe, if we had gotten some of the new things I ask for instead of you taking all of the money, we wouldn't have had this problem."

By this time the whole chemistry class was standing behind Mr. Hatsker, and the whole yearbook class was standing behind Mrs. Kay, and we looked like two armies facing off for battle.

"You don't know what real troubles are," Mrs. Kay replied. "We have spent half of the year taking pictures for the yearbook, and we were in the dark room developing them when your play school chemistry experiment drove us out. Do you know what happens when those negatives are exposed to light before they are ready?"

Before Mr. Hatsker could reply, Brent did. "A person gets a better picture than the one you guys usually take?"

I think Brent said it trying to be funny, or to diffuse the situation, but, suddenly, Mrs. Kay and her whole class turned and looked at us like we had a death wish or something. Brent's grin suddenly disappeared, and I think he realized, for the first time, that they outnumbered us three to one.

"Maybe you can just retake the pictures," Mr. Hatsker said, sounding somewhat apologetic.

"That is easier said than done," Mrs. Kay retorted. "Many of the sports teams and clubs have finished for the year."

We eventually returned to our classroom, and were happy to be away from the confrontation. The yearbook class started the arduous task of retaking all of the pictures, and everyone did their best to cooperate. They worked hard, and the yearbook came out right on schedule. But there was one picture they never did retake.

The chemistry club picture was conspicuously absent from the yearbook that year.

I woke with a start, and my heart was pounding. My wife, Donna, drowsily woke beside me and put a hand on my trembling arm. "Is something wrong?"

I swung my feet out of bed and sat up, trying to clear my head. "I just had a horrible nightmare that was so real."

"What was it?" she asked.

"I dreamed I was in a theater, and someone handed me a script and told me that I was to perform in a play in ten minutes. I had never even looked at the script before, but was shoved out onto the stage to improvise as best I could."

"What a strange dream."

"Yes," I replied. "I'm happy to wake and find out it wasn't real."

That morning, as I hurried to our normal routine, I was just putting pancakes on the griddle when the phone rang. Donna answered it, spoke briefly, and then turned to me. "The community is putting on *A Christmas Carol* and wondered if you would help."

The memory of the dream immediately returned. "I am willing to help with tech and stuff, but, after that dream, I think I'll forgo acting."

My children decided to try out, and all received parts, but I only helped with mundane set issues. On opening night I was on my way to the theater when I received a call from my daughter. Vandals had broken into the costume room and drew all over the boys' white shirts with red lipstick. "Dad, is there anything you can do?"

I hurried to the local thrift store and purchased every white boys' dress shirt they had - about 30 of them. When I arrived at the theater, the boys were desperately trying to clean their shirts and were happy to see what I had. Though the styles weren't quite right, and the sizes didn't all match, they were able to make do.

I settled into the audience by Donna to watch the night's

performance. Everything went well until the ghost of Christmas present entered the stage. He staggered about and stumbled through his lines. He barely appeared in the first act, having most of his performance in the second, so it was soon intermission.

As lights came up, I stood to stretch my legs and visit with those around me. The director approached and spoke in a desperate tone. "The boy that plays the ghost of Christmas present just passed out from working with the cleanser on the shirts." She shoved a script into my hand. "You're the only one I know that can do this on short notice, so you're on in 10 minutes."

I stood there in shock as I saw her disappear back to the stage. Donna nudged me, trying to get me to pull myself together. "Honey, you better hurry."

"But what about my dream?"

She just shrugged. "Look at it as a chance to prove it wrong."

I reviewed the lines the best I could and took my script on stage with me. But when the lights came up I couldn't read it anyway and discarded it. I then performed the most improvised role of my life.

When my part ended, I slipped back to my seat by Donna. "That was incredible," she whispered. I felt my performance was anything but incredible, and was sure she was just being nice.

When the play ended and the bows finished, the director, with a brief explanation, asked me to stand and take a bow. People cheered loudly, spurred on by the cast. But, with how I felt about my performance, I would have preferred to stay anonymous.

Donna hugged me, and I sighed heavily. "I'm just glad the nightmare is over."

That was when the director appeared, shoved a script into my hand again, and said, "The boy that plays Marley just had an attack of appendicitis, so you're on for the rest of the play."

And that's when I learned that sometimes nightmares can play out more than once.

Giving Away Christmas

I was working on a humorous Christmas story when the news came about the massacre of 20 children in Connecticut, along with the deaths of many adults that gave their lives to protect the children in their care. My two youngest daughters are about the same ages as some of the children that were killed, and I was too stunned to continue writing. Later in the afternoon, I went to my daughters' concert. When it ended, I hugged them tightly, grateful for their safety, while, at the same time, my heart ached for those who had lost people they loved.

When I finally sat back down to work on my story, my emotions were such that I knew I could never finish it this year. Instead, my thoughts turned to the real meaning of Christmas and a different story.

We had been out of graduate school a couple of years, and had paid down our student loans. We decided we could finally afford some of the gifts that our little girls really wanted. We told them they could make a list, and let them look through some catalogs. But, soon, they were overcome by the commercialism of the season.

Through the years of school, when we had very little money, our Christmases were simple, but family centered, and the strength we drew from the season, and from each other, couldn't be purchased at any price. I found myself longing for those same feelings as our little girls fretted more and more about what they wanted.

Finally, as the "I want" attitudes seemed to reach a crescendo, I decided it was time for a change. I called a family council. "This year," I said, "we are going to give away Christmas."

"Give away Christmas?" my oldest daughter asked.

"Yes. You will still get to choose some things, but they won't be for you. They will be for a child your age that has greater needs than you have."

My wife, Donna, and I had contacted the university for the address of a struggling young family who had children that were the same ages as our girls. What we purchased would go to them.

I was surprised at the eagerness my daughters showed for this. They spent even more time happily trying to pick out the perfect presents. They each purchased a set of clothes, a nice coat, and two toys that they would have loved for themselves. Donna and I purchased warm clothes for the parents. We also bought a full Christmas dinner with a turkey and everything to go with it. We added a large box of oranges and baskets of fruits and cookies.

It seemed to our little girls that Christmas Eve would never arrive, and they marked the days off on the calendar. When it finally came, we loaded everything into our old car and drove to the rundown apartment complex where the family lived. Donna insisted on playing Santa to deliver everything, even though the apartment was on the third floor.

It took her three trips, hauling the heavy boxes and stacking them next to the apartment door. We had our car windows open, and our little girls were listening intently. When they heard their mother's loud knocking on the door, and heard her feet pounding down the stairs, they squealed with excitement. Donna had just arrived out of breath at our car when we heard the squeaking of a door opening and heard the joyous delight of children's voices. Then, through the night, we heard a young mother's voice, full of emotion and in a strong southern accent, call out, "Thank you!"

Donna and our girls almost simultaneously yelled back, "You're welcome."

The next day we opened our few presents, played card games, built a snowman, and went sledding. In the evening we settled down with hot chocolate, and I read stories to my daughters. We talked about how the Christmas season is really about love, friends, and family, just as it was two millennia ago, when a wonderful baby became the newest member of a special family.

As we finished the stories, my daughters snuggled up in my arms as we watched the lights on the tree. Eventually, my oldest daughter broke the silence. "Daddy, I want to give away Christmas again next year."

"Me, too," I said. "Me, too."

As I think of the people in Connecticut, and know we have little to offer compared to what was taken away, I realize we can still give our love and prayers, and that we will do so.

Uncle Hickory's New Year's Resolution

Uncle Hickory made a New Year's resolution. He swore he would quit drinking. He had been driving while he was drunk and had one of the biggest scares of his life. He claimed the angel of death had come for him. He was trembling as he told us about it.

He had been to a New Year's Eve party, and the celebration was quite lively. There were many kinds of alcohol, and Uncle Hickory was hard pressed to find one he didn't like. He sampled all of them, from the lightest beer to the hardest vodka. Of course, he claimed he only had a little of each.

Once the old year had rolled away, and everyone had toasted the new one, it was time to head for home. Uncle Hickory wobbled his way to his car, feeling happy and light, hardly noticing the cold at all.

It had snowed heavily the previous two days, and, while they had been celebrating, the wind had kicked up, causing huge drifts. Uncle Hickory's old car plowed through the drifts, sliding back and forth as he went.

"Suddenly the road smoothed out," Uncle Hickory said, "and the car quit bucking and sliding. That was when it happened. I was traveling carefully along at about 30 miles per hour when I saw him approaching in my rear view mirror. He was floating toward me, all draped in black, closing the distance between us quickly."

Uncle Hickory shook visibly as he continued. "I knew who he was, and I knew he was coming for me. Even though it was slick and dangerous, I gunned the engine. I reached 50 miles per hour, and then looked in my rear view mirror. The gap between us was still getting smaller."

Uncle Hickory took some deep breaths, trying to calm himself. "As he was almost on my bumper, I put the pedal to the floor, rather to die from a wreck than to have that ghostly demon take me away. The speedometer climbed to 80 then to 90. I looked straight ahead, afraid to take my eyes off of the road. Finally, I glanced in my rear view mirror and no longer saw him. I felt a surge of relief flood over me when . . . "

Uncle Hickory paused, the blood draining from his face as the memory came back. We all leaned forward, anxious for the rest of the story.

"Just at the moment I thought I'd lost him," he continued, "there was a knock on my window. I turned, and there he was right by my door. I looked at my speedometer, and it said I was going more than 100 miles per hour, and still he stayed right there. I knew at that point I only had one chance."

"What?" we asked.

"What?" he responded. "I'll tell you what. I slammed on the brakes and then tore my way across the car and out the passenger side. I plowed through the snow and across the field, running for the light of a house I could see in the distance. I never looked back until I made it safely there. Once inside, I looked over my shoulder, and he was gone."

A few days later, Bart, a friend of mine, stopped to visit with me. "By the way, how is your Uncle Hickory?"

"He's okay," I answered. "Why do you ask?"

"Well, I was driving home New Year's day after working the night shift, and I saw his car off the road, stuck deep in a field. I got out to check on him, and the closer I got the harder he gunned his engine. When I got right up beside his car, I knocked on his window. When I did, he screamed and tore out the other side of his car and took off running across the field."

Bart paused, the concern showing in his face. "I tried to catch up to him, but I've never seen anyone run that fast, and I finally gave up. I just wanted to make sure he made it home safely."

"He did," I replied. "But if we keep this just between you and me, he just might remain sober."

Playing To Win

I am not a gamer, and I doubt I ever could be. I was a math and computer science major, and I have always found myself more interested in how programs worked, and trying to outsmart a game, rather than actually playing it.

But if there is one thing that I am, it is competitive. Thus, even though I've never been into playing video games, when my wife, Donna, claims she can beat me at one, I take it very seriously.

One night when we were newly married, Donna challenged me to a game of *Tombstone City*. I told her I didn't think I had time because I had a lot of homework to do. She just laughed, knowing my lack of expertise. "That's okay. It will probably take less than five minutes for the tumbleweeds to get you anyway."

Tombstone City was a game on an old TI computer that someone had given us. The computer connected to our television, which basically didn't have any other use, since it usually didn't pick up a TV signal anyway.

In *Tombstone City*, tumbleweeds would come after the character on the screen of the person that was playing. If they hit him, he died. But if he shot the tumbleweed before it got him, the tumbleweed turned into a tombstone. The tombstones became permanent, and the tumbleweeds were forced to go around them.

A person received points in two different ways. First, 10 points came for each tumbleweed that was shot. Second, a person received one point for each minute their character survived the onslaught of the tumbleweeds. Surviving became harder and harder as the tumbleweeds came faster and faster.

I told Donna that I would take her challenge and told her to go first, while I continued to study. Donna has very good reflexes and her turn lasted about ten minutes. She racked up about 700 points, knocking off a lot of tumbleweeds. When she finished, she grinned at me. "See if you can beat that!"

She went off to check on dinner, and I sat down to play. I moved my player into the center and waited for the tumbleweeds to come to me. As they did, I fired at them until I had created a circle of tombstones around my player so that the tumbleweeds couldn't get through to him. I then went back to my studies.

Donna came into the room and saw me studying again. She glanced at the screen and laughed. "You only made 62 points? Six tumbleweeds and two minutes have got to be a new record low, even for you."

I smiled back at her. "You might want to note that the game is not over yet. I'm still playing."

"What do you mean? You're back at your studies."

"Look at the screen," I replied.

She looked and saw the game was not over and that I had just gained my 63rd point for lasting another minute. Knowing me, she went over and studied the screen carefully to figure out what I had done. When she finally realized that I had enclosed myself in tombstones so that the tumbleweeds couldn't get to me, she spoke in exasperation. "What kind of a game strategy is that?"

"I am getting one point for every minute," I told her. "It will only take me a little more than 11 hours to equal your score, and then I will continue to surpass it. I figure I can just let it keep running forever."

"That's cheating," she replied.

"If you don't want to get beat," I told her, "you should learn not to challenge the master."

And that was when Donna, as master of the power cord, pulled the plug on the computer.

A Geek's Guide To A High Score

When my wife, Donna, and I were first married, we were given an old TI computer. The games on it were very limited, but so were our finances.

I was majoring in both computer science and mathematics, and had very little time for any outside activities. Donna was happy to have any time I could share with her. Often this included playing a game on that old computer called Exploding Bananas.

In this game, two giant, King Kong sized apes each climbed a different skyscraper. Then, controlled by the people playing the game, the apes threw exploding bananas at each other. The goal was to blow out a wedge in the opponents building so that it tipped over before yours did. Basically, it was a precursor to Angry Birds.

One day we were given a new game. It was a math game where numbers fell from the sky and had a math operation between them: addition, subtraction, multiplication, or division. A person had to type in the correct value before it hit the ground, or they stacked up, ending the game when the numbers reached the top of the screen.

Though Donna has never played a lot of games, she enjoyed this one and was getting very good at it. She had gotten up to around 2,000 points on it, an incredible score. That was when she challenged me to see if I could do better. After doing math all day, the last thing I wanted to do was more math. But she kept teasing me about it, and I finally decided to take her challenge. But I was programming in machine code at the time, and I chose to deal with her challenge differently than she expected.

One day, while she was away at the grocery store, I turned the computer on and played a very short game, only gaining 23 points before letting the computer finish off the game and record my score. My 23 points looked stupid compared to her 2,000, but it gave me what I needed.

I went in and copied the machine code file for the score to a backup in case I made a mistake. I then looked through the bits of the original program file, searching for our names represented in binary ASCII code bytes of ones and zeros. Once I found them, I analyzed the bytes around them and determined which bytes represented my score and which bytes represented hers.

By changing the bits in my score appropriately, I gave myself the highest score possible of 2,147,483,647. By changing hers, I gave her a score of -1.

Once they were changed, I saved the file. It was time to check and see if it did what I expected. I turned on the game, and the scores were just as I planned. Now was the hardest part, not giving away that I had done something while I waited for her to play the game.

Donna returned home from shopping, and it was all I could do to keep myself from grinning while I continued to study. Finally came the moment when she sat down to play. When the screen with the previous games' scores popped up at the beginning, she gasped. She spun around and glared at me. "What did you do?"

"I beat your score," I answered calmly.

"But how did you get a score that high?" she asked.

"I'm just good at math," I answered.

"Yeah, right," she replied sarcastically. "And I know it's impossible to get a negative score playing the game, so how come mine is negative?"

"You're just special," I teased.

She then demanded I tell her what I had done. When I finished, she said, "If you want dinner tonight, you better change it back, right now!"

And I did, though I still retained the highest score for creativity.

We Are All God's Children

I was with the youngest primary children at church last Sunday, when something happened that made me think about Civil Rights Day and the challenges this country has faced. One of the teachers was trying to help the children understand that God loves everyone, no matter who they are, and that we should be kind to everybody, even if they are different from us. She showed a picture of a little Down Syndrome girl and asked the children if they could see any differences between her and themselves.

One little girl raised her hand. "Yes," she said. "She's smiling."

"Yes, she is smiling," the teacher replied. "But, can you see anything else that makes her different from you?"

The children looked and looked and strained to see a difference. Finally, another little girl raised her hand. When the teacher called on her, she said, "She's dressed in summer clothes instead of big, thick winter clothes." No matter how long the teacher asked them about the difference, the children could not see anything of importance.

I smiled as I thought of an experience with my own little daughter, Elliana. When she was five years old, she was invited over to play at the home of a family that was new to the area. The mother, father, and their four biological children were all Caucasian, blue-eyed, and very blond. They also had a sweet little African American daughter that they had adopted.

My wife, Donna, had grown up in Los Angeles, and had lots of friends from other races and nationalities. I lived in New York for a time and grew to love people from almost every religion and region of the world. But our children had not had any such opportunities. The culture here in Idaho is not very diverse. Donna was concerned that our daughter might be surprised at the mix in the family, and innocently say something she should not. So she simply told her that one child in the family was adopted.

"What does 'dopted mean?" Elliana asked.

"Well, when a child is adopted into a family, they are not born to the mother of that family, but to another mother," Donna replied. "But if that child's mother can't take care of them, the other family takes the child into their home and loves them as their own."

This was not really a new concept to Elliana, as we had been foster parents before, so she smiled and said, "That is so nice."

Elliana went over there and played most of the day. There were four girls and one boy in the family. The girls played dolls with Elliana and did lots of girl things, but when they all played soccer in the back yard, the little boy joined them. They had lunch, and cake for dessert, and all sorts of good things.

When Elliana arrived home, we asked her how it went. "It was the most fun ever," she said. "They have really pretty dolls, and we played soccer in their great, big yard."

Then Elliana stopped and looked at her mother. "Momma, which one in their family was 'dopted?"

"Well, did you notice that one child was a bit different from the others?" Donna asked.

Elliana thought for a moment, and then she smiled. "Oh, yes, there was one that was different."

"And what was the difference?" Donna asked.

Donna hoped to make this a teaching moment, sharing with our daughter about how wonderfully diverse people are. But, instead, we were the ones that learned. We learned that children aren't born with ideas of differences, but it is something we build in our hearts as we grow older.

For, in answer to the question, Elliana just laughed and said, "It's obvious, Momma. One was a boy."

A Reluctant Dancer

When I was a teenager, my church leader called me into his office. "Daris, do you remember the announcement about the statewide dance festival?" I nodded, so he continued. "I need you to participate."

I told him I wasn't a good dancer, and I often had other commitments, but he just smiled and said, "I'm sure you'll do fine."

I went the next Tuesday and learned that all of the girls had volunteered, but each boy had only reluctantly agreed, after being asked. We were assigned partners according to size. I was to dance with Yolanda. She was the biggest girl, and I was the strongest boy.

The dance instructor soon became frustrated with us boys. We were all farm workers and danced with the grace of old plow horses. We wore big work boots, and the girls' feet were suffering. Our instructor finally demanded we all take our shoes off. Farm boys hate removing their boots, but, eventually, we complied.

I did my best, and even though I felt awkward, I enjoyed it. I may not have been a great dancer, but I was strong and could do the lifts easily. Yolanda was pretty, but, because she was bigger than most girls, she hadn't had a lot of dance opportunities. She was kind and forgiving of my inadequacies.

The dancing went fairly well until a point where the girls jumped into our arms and we then dropped them onto their feet in front of us. Ted dropped Alice perfectly, except that the horns on the bull on his belt buckle caught her dress and ripped it from the hem all the way to her waist. The instructor ordered us boys from the room, saying that practice was over.

We practiced for a few more weeks, and then I missed one for a track meet. The week after that we danced to the point I had learned, and as everyone else continued, I turned to see what they were doing. The girls all dropped backwards, and the boys caught them. But I was facing the other way and wasn't ready, and Yolanda fell on her back at my feet. She wasn't hurt, landing against me on the way down, but I felt horrible and tried to apologize and help her up.

It seemed to be the last straw for the instructor. She yelled right in my face. "You will never be able to dance right! Get out, and don't come back!"

I quickly left the room. I felt horrible about Yolanda falling, and I was humiliated and embarrassed. I climbed onto my bicycle and sped the four miles home. I had just started my chores when the instructor showed up, coming right into the barn to speak to me.

"Daris, I'm sorry," she said. "I know it wasn't your fault, and I shouldn't have said what I said. Won't you please come back?" I told her that I felt it would be better if she just got someone else.

The next week, shortly after the dance practice ended, the instructor came again. When she asked me once more to come back, I refused, but this time she had brought Yolanda. Yolanda pleaded with me, looking at me with her big brown eyes. "If you don't come back," she said, "I won't get to dance. None of the other boys will dance with me." I hesitated, but I finally nodded.

I came the next week, but was three weeks behind. Feelings of inadequacy plagued me, but I worked hard and Yolanda patiently taught me. When the performance came and we joined the thousands of other dancers on the football field, I felt I did okay.

As our final number ended, the other girls hurried off together, but Yolanda hung back by me. When we were somewhat alone, she grabbed my hand and pulled me to face her.

"Thank you, Daris, for coming back and dancing with me."

"Thank you for being patient with me," I said. "I'm sorry I'm not a better dancer."

"You are something far more important," she said, "you are kind."

She hugged me and then ran to catch the other girls, leaving me to think about what truly is most important.

A Dancer With Too Much Class

My daughter stared at my college transcript. "Dad, did you really take social dance?"

I smiled as I remembered back to that morning on the first day of the semester when a friend, Sherry, knocked on my apartment door. When I opened it, she smiled. "You are just the person I was looking for. Will you take a dance class with me?"

"Sherry," I replied, "I have a full schedule, and I am a horrible dancer."

"Oh, come on," she said. "I'll help you, and the instructor said a girl can't add in now without having a boy sign up with her."

I felt my tension level increase as I remembered my past dance failures. But she smiled and looked at me with her big brown eyes, and despite all common sense, my mental reasoning failed, and I said yes.

"I've already had the teacher sign our add/drop cards," she said, handing me one. "All you have to do is sign yours, and I'll take them to the registration office."

I signed, and later that day we went to the class. We quickly found out the reason a girl had to bring a boy. There were 54 girls and 8 boys. Sherry leaned over and whispered to me. "I'm not taking a dance class that is mostly girls. Let's drop it at the end of the hour."

I nodded my agreement as the teacher started to explain about the class. "Welcome to Social Dance 204, fourth semester dance."

I leaned over to Sherry. "Fourth? I thought it was first semester." She just shrugged.

The instructor continued. "Since this is the final class of the sequence, you will all be expected to know the 12 major dance forms and compete in them. As a final, we will have an in-class competition. Every couple may compete at the regional dance competition, if desired, but the couple winning the in-class competition is required to represent us. Your grade will be based on how well you compete."

I could feel my heart pounding at the thought of competition. I was sure glad we were dropping. When the instructor finished talking, it was time to dance. "Let's start with something lively," he said. "Cha Cha, everyone."

"Sherry," I whispered, "I don't have a clue what the Cha Cha is."

"Just follow what I do," she whispered back.

I tried to follow, but she was stepping so fast. She would turn in, so I would turn in, but by the time I did, she was turning out. At one point my foot caught her ankle, and she started to fall. I tried to catch her, but, instead, we both went down. Everyone else giggled, and I wished I could disappear. As I helped her to her feet, she said, "Perhaps we shouldn't wait until the end of the class to sign out."

While the others continued dancing, we went to the instructor. "This isn't going to work for us to be in this class," Sherry told him, "so we would like to sign out."

We always carried extra add/drop cards the first few days of class, so she handed him hers, and he signed it. I held mine out to him, and he didn't even pretend he would take it. Instead he said, "I'm sorry, but I don't sign boys out of the class. You are in for the semester."

"But I've never even had first semester dance," I said, "let alone second or third."

"I'll try to remember that when I do grades," he answered.

"But I'm horrible at dancing," I said.

"I can see that," he replied. "That's all the more reason you need this class."

"It's not fair that . . . " I started to complain, but he interrupted me.

"I would suggest you find a girl to dance with, and start

dancing. You've got a lot to learn."

I looked at Sherry. "I'm sorry," she said, and she quickly left.

As the instructor stepped to the microphone to announce the next dance, and I stood there feeling scared and apprehensive, a young lady tapped me on the shoulder. I turned to look at her. She was a nice looking girl, and she smiled pleasantly. "Hi, I'm Ginny. I heard your dilemma. I'd be happy to dance with you, if you want."

I nodded, she reached out her hand, and together we went to the dance floor.

As the memory faded, I turned back to my daughter. "Yeah, it's hard to believe, but your clumsy old dad actually signed up for a social dance class."

Competing In Dance And A Change Of Heart

Class was ending as our instructor informed us, "Since we only have two weeks of class left, next time we will begin the competition to see which couple will represent us at the regional ballroom championships."

As he spoke, my mind went back to what had brought me to this point. My friend, Sherry, needed a partner in order to sign into the college dance class. At our first class there were 54 girls and 8 boys. Sherry dropped out, but the teacher refused to sign my drop card because he needed male class members. To make matters worse, it was fourth semester dance, and I had never had the first three. When he first announced that our grade would be based on how well we competed in class and the ballroom championships, I figured I would fail for sure.

But then Ginny came to my rescue. The first class was a disaster. Everyone else knew all of the dances, but I knew next to nothing. I tried to follow her, but I did horribly. We were supposed to trade partners every time, but few other girl would dance with me, and after I had crashed into other couples for about the fifth time, the instructor allowed Ginny to take me to an empty part of the ballroom and teach me from the beginning.

She was patient and kind, and I gradually started to learn. As class ended, she suggested that, besides class twice a week, I should come to the three weekly evening dances.

"But, Ginny, can't I learn enough to pass by just practicing in class?" I asked.

"Maybe," she answered. "But what about the competition? Don't you want to win?"

I shook my head. "I just want to pass the class."

Ginny's eyes filled with tears, and she left. At the next class, she was quiet, but kindly taught me. Though she was patient, she wasn't happy, and I knew it was because of my attitude about the competition.

As the class ended, I asked, "Ginny, why does winning mean so much to you?"

She spoke quietly as she answered. "My best friend, David, and I were dance partners from the time we were in first grade. We took the first three semesters of dance together and hoped to win the regional ballroom championship."

"I'm sure he must be way better than I am," I said. "Why doesn't he join the class so the two of you can practice?"

Ginny couldn't hold back the tears. "He was killed in a car wreck three weeks ago heading home for Christmas break. I had hoped to win this for him, but I can't do it alone."

She turned and quickly left, leaving me standing there feeling like a jerk.

It seemed like forever until the next class. When she came in, I hurried to meet her. "I was afraid you might not come back."

"Even if we don't compete to win," she replied, "I thought you might need me."

"Ginny," I said, "I definitely need you. And I may never be as good as David, but that shouldn't stop me from trying. If you will help me, I promise to do my best."

She smiled. "Then let the training begin."

We practiced hard at our classes along with three evenings each week. Ginny had an eye for detail, and even had me practice being more graceful while escorting her to the dance floor.

"You walk like a bowlegged cowboy," she said.

"I am a bowlegged cowboy," I replied.

"That doesn't mean you have to walk like one."

I began to dance well with her, but, when the instructor made all of us switch partners, I felt awkward and made lots of mistakes.

Ginny scolded me. "What's the matter? You know the dance."

"It feels awkward and different with someone else," I replied.

"Well, if you want to be a champion, you better get so you

54

can dance with any girl."

I continued to work, and Ginny continued to coach me, and, soon, I was dancing well with each partner. But more importantly, I found a change of heart. Ginny had become my friend, and a friend matters more than a grade does. As our instructor announced the beginning of the competition, I knew what I wanted now was to do my best for her.

Learning To Believe In Yourself

I was a horrible dancer, and I mistakenly signed into a fourth semester college dance class. I hadn't had the first three, yet the instructor refused to sign my drop card because he needed male participants. But worst of all, we had to compete in a dance competition for our final grade.

Ginny kindly said she would teach me. At first I only hoped to pass the class. But when I realized how much it meant to her to win to honor her best friend and former dance partner, who had died in a car wreck, I put my heart into it.

When we reached the last two weeks of class, the in-class competition began. Ginny told me I needed to wear my best suit. "Part of the elegance of dance is in how you dress," she said, so on that day, I went to her apartment to have her see if I passed inspection.

She frowned when she saw me. "Do you ever shine your shoes?"

"Not too often," I admitted.

She straightened my tie, had me tuck my shirt in better, and helped me polish my shoes. When she was satisfied, she left to curl her hair and change into her dress. When she came back into the living room and smiled at me, I said, "Ginny, you're beautiful." She blushed as she reached out and took my arm so I could escort her to class.

At the end of each class period, the teacher would decide who would continue on. The couples who were not in ballroom attire on the first day were out. By the last class, only two couples were left. We were one of them. We danced all 12 dances with everyone else judging. When the teacher announced Ginny and me as the winners, everyone else broke into loud applause.

Shaking my hand, he said, "On that first day, when I saw you stumble around the floor, I would never have believed you could win."

We had a few more days of private coaching from the teacher before the big event. On the competition day, I again met Ginny at her apartment. After I passed inspection, we headed to the large gym where the competition was to be held. We hadn't gone too far when Ginny stopped and pulled me to face her.

"Daris, you're trembling horribly."

"Ginny," I said, "I'm scared to death. I've never done anything like this. I'm used to power and strength in athletic competition, not elegance."

She squeezed my hand. "You have it in you whether you believe it or not. And you've worked so hard. I want you to know that, no matter what happens, I'm proud of you."

We arrived at the huge gym, checked in, then sat in the seats with the other competitors. Soon the whole room filled with spectators - thousands of them. When it was time to begin, hundreds of couples packed the floor. As we all danced, the judges walked around. If they tapped a couple's shoulders, that couple was out. After an hour, we had danced the full repertoire of 12 dances, and only 20 couples were left. We were one of them.

By then I was really trembling. Ginny squeezed my hand. "You can do it; just take a deep breath."

By the time we had danced all 12 dances again, there were only three couples left. We were still in. After a couple more songs, it was just us and one other couple. We danced two more dances, and still the judges couldn't decide. The crowd had grown so loud we could hardly hear the music, but Ginny and I danced the next dance flawlessly. When we finished, the judges consulted, and the head judge stepped to the microphone. "After watching the performance of these two couples, we have decided to declare a tie." The crowd cheered wildly.

They only had two medals, so they gave one to each couple. Ginny handed me ours. "You've worked so hard that this should be yours."

"No, Ginny," I said as I slipped it around her neck. "It's yours."

She smiled as I continued. "What I received was greater than any medal. I've had the friendship of someone who cared enough to help me believe in myself so I could become more than I ever thought possible. That is the greatest reward I could ever have."

A Valentine Description

Valentine's Day was on Saturday that year, so a women's group in the area decided to have a social for married couples. They would have three, one hour sessions in the morning with speakers sharing how men and women differ. Afterward, there would be a luncheon where we could all sit around and visit.

My wife, Donna, showed me the flier. "Would you like to go?" she asked.

"I have an idea," I said, after I finished reading it. "Why don't they have them speak about how men and women are the same? That would only take about ten minutes, and that would leave a lot more time for the luncheon."

"Very funny," she replied.

While we were still talking about whether we would be going, the phone rang. When Donna answered it, the person on the other end asked her if she would play the piano for the social. That clinched it. We had to attend.

As I checked my schedule, I found I had some other commitments early Saturday morning. Even though I would be able to be there for most of it, I would have to be late.

"When you get there, you will come up and sit by me on the stand won't you?" Donna asked. "After all, it is Valentine's Day."

"If I get there late, I don't want to make a big commotion," I answered. "I think I will just slip in the back, and then join you between sessions."

She looked at me with big puppy dog eyes. "But that won't be very romantic."

"But, Honey, you know how much I hate people staring at me," I said. "And if I have to go clear up on the stand . . . "

She stopped me. "Let's do this. I will have someone save a couple of seats on the front row, and I will come down off of the stand and join you." I thought about it a minute and felt that was a fair compromise.

Saturday came, and things didn't go as planned. I was even later than I expected. When I messaged Donna to say I was on my way, she texted back that she had to play for some extra musical numbers and couldn't join me immediately. "But I talked a lady on the first row into saving us a couple of seats," she said.

"How will I know which seats are ours?" I asked.

"That's easy," she replied. "The room is packed. There are only two front row seats left."

"How will the lady know it's me?" I asked.

"I described you to her, so it will be fine," Donna's text said.

When I arrived, I looked through the door, and, indeed, found a packed room. I stood in the back and could only see two seats right on the front row. I made my way up there, trying not to draw attention to myself. When I sat down, the lady leaned over and whispered to me. "I'm sorry, but these seats are reserved for someone else."

Embarrassed, I looked for other seats at the front, but couldn't see any. So, with everyone staring at me, I made my way to the back again. Between sessions, Donna found me. She led me up to the same seats I had left. She introduced me to the lady that had told me the seats were reserved, and then Donna went to take her place at the piano. The lady whispered an apology.

When the meetings ended, Donna and I were finally able to talk. "By the way," I asked, "how did you describe me to the lady that was saving the seats?"

"Oh, I just told her you were super, amazingly handsome," Donna said.

"That was the problem then," I told her.

"What was the problem?" Donna asked.

"She told me she didn't recognize me from your description."

Competing With Confidence

Our high school wrestling team was gathering to board the bus when Coach came out of his office. He walked over to me. "Howard, Hardy has the flu. You're replacing him on varsity tonight."

I felt a rush of adrenaline. I was a freshman, and this would be my first varsity match. Coach spoke sternly to me. "I know the guy they have in your weight, and he's the worst wrestler on their varsity squad. You should be able to take him easily."

"Yeah," Gould said, "Hardy has pinned him every time they've wrestled, usually in the first round."

"If the matches go like I expect," Coach added, "the score will be tight. We really need a pin out of you." I nodded, as my heart started to pound, not wanting to disappoint my team.

My teammates continued to talk about how easy this would be for me. I was excited to think that my first varsity match would likely be a win, and maybe a pin.

That evening, as the competition proceeded, the matches were evenly split. By the time it was my match, we were down by five. Coach grabbed me by my headgear. "We've got to have a win, and we really need a pin. Go after him."

The second the whistle blew, I shot in and took him down. I thought the match was mine, but we no sooner hit the mat than things changed. He moved quickly and reversed me. Back and forth we fought in one of the toughest matches I have ever wrestled. When the first round ended, he was ahead six to four. Coach yelled, "Howard, what's your problem! Hardy would have pinned him by now!"

In the second round my opponent increased his lead. In the third round I fought like a lion, afraid of what my teammates would say if I lost, and I started to come back. With only twenty seconds to go, he was ahead 11 to 10. I shot in and fought for a takedown. I took him to the mat, but the buzzer sounded on our way down, and I received no points. I had lost.

As I walked from the mat, discouraged, Coach blasted me, swearing and cursing. "Howard, you probably cost us a win! I doubt you'll ever wrestle varsity for me again!"

My teammates also said many derogatory things to me. Luckily, we won the next three matches, and our team won by one point. When we climbed on the bus, it was suggested by my varsity teammates that I should sit at the front away from them. When coach came on, he reiterated that our win was lucky. Then he said, "We can't expect to win as a team when we lose the easy matches, huh, Howard?" I just nodded and looked out the window.

The next week was a big tournament. Hardy was back, and his first opponent was the one I had lost to. Coach grabbed me. "Now, Howard, watch Hardy and see how it's supposed to be done."

Hardy confidently walked out onto the mat. Within thirty seconds after the whistle blew, he was pinned. Coach stood there in shock as the opposing team's coach came over. "You really gave us a scare last week when your wrestler nearly beat Barton. When Barton moved here a couple of weeks ago, we were excited to learn that he is a two-time state champion and has pinned every opponent he has wrestled in the past two years. When he nearly lost to your wrestler, and we found out his opponent was only a freshman, today's rematch was all the team has talked about." He paused a moment and pointed at me. "So why isn't he wrestling varsity today?"

Coach was so stunned that he just shrugged. My teammates were shocked. When one senior was finally able to speak, he said, "Howard, we all owe you an apology. If he had pinned you last week, we would have lost."

Later that year, after the state tournament, when I learned that Barton had pinned all of his other opponents, I wondered how well I would have done against him if I had really known how good he was. But I did smile, remembering that I was the only one to ruin his perfect pin record.

Never Old

I was in my early 20's, living in Medina, New York, a small town with a substantial immigrant population. I rented my apartment there from Mrs. Kazowski, a sweet older lady.

I originally shared that apartment with another young man, Hangstrom, with whom I worked. Mrs. Kazowski had raised her family, and they were all a long distance away, so she treated us much like sons. She kept her days busy with many things, but in the quiet evening she grew lonely. For that reason, she almost always asked us to join her for dinner. She did it so much that we started contributing to the cost of her grocery bill.

Dinner every night consisted of stuffed cabbage rolls, the main staple from her home country. During my months there I felt as though I ate enough of them to keep that whole cabbage industry in business.

Hangstrom was always okay with us eating with Mrs. Kazowski, even though he hated stuffed cabbage rolls. But when she would ask us if we wanted to go someplace with her, he always had a ready excuse.

Then Hangstrom left, and I ended up working with another young man, Stanton. It was shortly after he arrived that Mrs. Kazowski asked us to attend a Christmas program with her in a town about 30 miles away. I didn't know the reason for Hangstrom's reluctance, so Stanton and I accepted.

As we drove along, everything was going okay until we reached the outskirts of town and turned onto the narrow two lane highway. Suddenly, Mrs. Kazowski gunned the big Oldsmobile forward so quickly that I swear that if I hadn't been wearing my seat belt I would have gone through the back window.

We quickly approached speeds rivaling the Autobahn, coming up fast on another car. The problem was that an old farm truck was approaching from the other direction. Instead of slowing, Mrs. Kazowski increased her speed. Stanton gasped and covered his head, preparing for impact. I sat, frozen, in my seat.

Just as we were almost right on the other car's bumper, she swung the wheel hard to the left. Our car went up onto two wheels, nearly on its side, in the soft gravel on the shoulder of the road. I'm sure the driver of the other car could look out his window and see the underside of ours as we passed.

We had no sooner passed the other car than Mrs. Kazowski swung us back into the lane in front of it. Stanton opened his eyes just as we were approaching another car. Still, Mrs. Kazowski didn't slow. This time, a huge pickup was coming from the other direction. It was farther away, and she accelerated. We passed, and both the car on our left and the pickup coming straight at us braked, giving just enough room for us to slide between them. From my vantage point, I could see the pickup's bumper inches from the side of our car.

As we approached the next car, we could see a little old couple in it. Though very few people ever went the posted 50 MPH speed limit, they were. Mrs. Kazowski cussed and then turned to us. "What do they think this is, a parking lot?"

Thankfully, nothing was coming from the other direction this time, and for the first time Mrs. Kazowski slowed. She rolled down her window as we pulled up alongside, and she yelled, "Geezers! Get off the road!"

Mrs. Kazowski, who was 85 years old, then turned to us. "I don't know why they let old people drive. They should lock them up in a nursing home."

When we finally arrived at the church where the Christmas program was to be held, and stepped out into the freezing December air, Stanton, who was nearly as white as the winter snow, leaned over and whispered to me.

"How long do you think it would take us to walk the 30 miles back to our apartment?"

What Students Learned In Math Class

Over the years, we have found that one of the students' greatest criticisms of any math class is their claim that they didn't learn anything. I, therefore, as part of their final, have the students list ten things that they have learned. These items can be anything at all in relation to the class. They are allowed to write their list ahead of time and bring it to the final, if they want. Most observations are quite normal, but some make for interesting reading. Each year I list some of them, and here is this year's list.

1) I learned that my friends and classmates are always willing to give me advice whether I want it or need it or not. And when they need some advice and I try to give them some, they act all annoyed.

2) I learned that what TV makes us believe about the fact that we'll all grow up and be millionaires, and our lives will be extraordinary, is bogus. If we work hard, our lives may be good but still just basically kind of normal, and only as good as the effort we put in.

3) I learned that calculators and their functions really save time. I just wish I had learned those time saving functions before I spent tons more time on my homework.

4) I learned that I learn better by paying more attention in class instead of just taking notes and not even knowing what I am writing about.

5) I realized that I should stick to music because math is not my forte.

6) I learned that my brother is terrible at math and I should never ask him for help. I'm better off doing it on my own.

7) I learned that with the right teaching techniques, I am actually intelligent in math, and it's no longer my worst subject.

8) I learned that procrastination is a horrible habit, and a person can get a lot more sleep if they stay ahead in their assignments.

9) I learned how fulfilling and great it feels to get an A on a math test.

10) I learned life without goals is like golf without holes. (I like that quote.)

11) From the section on logic, I learned all the things that were wrong with my arguments with my parents.

12) I learned that it is entirely possible to have a good teacher and enjoy the class and still hate the subject. You are a really good teacher. It's too bad you have to teach math.

13) I learned that there are at least two girls in our class that are both totally in love with me, and that makes it hard to focus. On math, anyway.

14) I learned that when March Madness is on, my grades go down.

15) When I think I can't afford a house, I can now do the calculation and then I will know for sure that I can't.

16) I learned that the girl I would marry sat in the row next to me, but I also learned I should have paid more attention in class instead of to her.

17) I learned how to survive college without eating Ramen noodles.

18) I learned how to see through trick questions. (Not that you had any, I'm just saying it.)

19) I learned that, if the teacher says you can have a note card in the exam, it is probably a good idea to get one ready and take it to the test.

20) I learned that people don't like it when you are trying to be funny and they are trying to pay attention to the teacher and learn something. They make you feel like you are annoying instead of funny.

21) I learned that I can always tell when Professor Howard's wife is away because his clothes don't match very well.

22) I have learned that the more painful something is, the more a person learns from it. I have learned more in this class than anything else I have ever done.

What To Look For In A College

My daughter was finishing her high school senior year when she expressed her desire to attend a certain university. I knew that the programs for which it was known would not be of interest to her, so I was confused at her choice.

"Why do you plan to go there?" I asked.

"For a couple of reasons," she replied. "First, they offered me a scholarship. And second, and most important, it is a long way from here, and I want to get away."

She seemed to think I would be surprised at the second statement, but I wasn't. I associate with thousands of students every year, and that happens to be a common criterion for their choice. But being her father, and being a man, I tend to take a more logical approach.

"Sweetheart," I said, "let's analyze your choice."

"Dad, you can't talk me out of it," she replied. "I know that the local university gave me great scholarships, but I don't want to stay here."

"I'm not saying you should," I said. "I just know that there are many things to consider, the first and foremost being the quality of your major program."

"I plan to major in music, and they have that," she replied.

"But I happen to know that it isn't highly rated," I told her, "although their engineering is."

Though I didn't want to talk her into any certain university, I was sure this wasn't a good match for her, and I did want her to think more about it. But the more we talked, the more she insisted that was where she would go.

Her mother wisely said, "I think we should visit there and check it out."

That university is a long day's drive away, so we worked out a plan for the trip. We arrived at our destination at 2:00 A.M. By

7:00 A.M. we were on campus so we could spend a full day there.

My wife had scheduled for us to see all of the important things pertaining to a music major. We watched their symphony practice. It was far from stellar. We attended a group lesson, and the instructor didn't show up, so the students had to teach each other. We looked at the number of music performances scheduled for the semester, and there were very few. Their music program didn't impress us, but her determination remained fixed.

We didn't like the student housing. The accommodations were antiquated. Some students told us the power kept going out because the breakers in the building kept blowing. They also said that many of the beds were so uncomfortable that they, instead, slept on the floor. Still, our daughter insisted that she would be going to that university.

We looked at possible employment for her and found next to nothing. We looked at public transportation for her, and there was none. The more we looked, the less I liked it. But she still insisted that was where she would go.

Our last stop was the student activity center. With the party reputation of the school, I was sure there would be plenty to excite a young girl, and in that I was correct. All of the activities that were scheduled impressed her. She just started to tell us once more that she would be going there, when a young man from our hometown walked in.

He was a boy just older than she, and the one she described as the most annoying boy in the school. He no sooner saw us than he came over to visit.

"What are you doing here?" he asked. When he found out about her plans to attend there, he smiled at her. "That is great! Then we can date!" The look on her face was priceless.

As we walked away, she turned to her mother and me. "I think I need to find a school that has a better music program."

And that was when I realized what was truly the most important consideration for choosing the right school to attend.

Hiding My Own Easter Eggs

One year, my daughter, Celese, invited us to come to her house for Easter weekend. She also invited my father-in-law and mother-in-law, John and Corky.

Whenever we are there, we always have a pizza party and movie night. I buy the pizza and rent whatever movie our grandchildren want. Celese and Jimmy get to leave their children in our care and have a night out together.

John and Corky also planned events. They wanted to have a big Easter egg hunt. They bought 96 plastic eggs, and lots of candy to fill them. John and I would have the privilege of hiding the eggs all around Celese and Jimmy's yard. Then my younger children and the grandchildren would get to hunt for them.

"You think you can find some good places to hide them?" John asked me.

"Not only can I find some great places to hide the eggs," I joked, "but with my memory the way it is, I could hide my own Easter eggs and never be able to find them all."

He laughed. "I'm sure you won't even need to worry about hunting. If there is candy in them, the children will find them."

For the movie, the grandchildren chose Veggie Tales. We cooked the pizza, made some lemonade, and sat down to veg out - literally. By the time it was over, my grandson was asleep in my arms, and my granddaughter was asleep against me. As I tucked them into bed, my granddaughter asked, "We didn't miss the Easter egg hunt, did we?"

"No," I answered, as I kissed her good night. "We will do that tomorrow."

We were still asleep the next morning when the grandchildren came in and pounced on us. "Is it time to hunt the

Easter eggs yet, Grandpa?" my granddaughter asked.

I told them that their mother said they had to have a good breakfast first. I knew I wasn't going to get any more sleep, so I got up and started cooking scrambled eggs and toast. Once we were done eating, it was all we could do to keep them inside while John and I hid the eggs.

We worked hard to find all of the best spots, and it took about 20 minutes to hide all of the eggs. We had just finished, and told the children they could hunt, when Corky stepped out of the motor home, holding a big bag of candy.

"John, have you seen the plastic eggs that I bought to fill with candy? I can't find them."

John glanced at me and then turned to her. "You didn't fill them?"

"No," she replied. "I was just getting ready to."

My grandson came over to me to show me a plastic egg he found, and I opened it, and sure enough, it was empty. We collected the ones the children had found, and shooed all of them back inside so that John and I could try to find the eggs we had hidden. When we finished, we totaled them, and including the ones the children had found, we only had 82. No matter how much we hunted, we couldn't find the other 14.

John grinned at me. "I guess you're right. We could hide our own Easter eggs and never ever find them."

Corky filled the ones we found, and John and I hid them again. The children hunted for them, and we had lots of fun. John and I kept a bag of candy with us, and when the children found one of the empty rogue eggs, we would take it and magically fill it for them. But then they began to realize that if they emptied the full ones and brought them back to us, we wouldn't know any better and would magically fill those, too. Pretty soon our bags of candy were empty and the children were all hyper.

We hadn't planned to give them all of the candy; it just worked out that way. My little granddaughter came and climbed on my lap so I could wash off the chocolate.

"Grandpa," she said, "I'm glad you're forgetful."

I smiled and hugged her. I guess every cloud has a silver lining.

A Blanket Permission To Dance

Lena felt like crying as she tried to reason with her mother. "I'm nearly 19 years old. Soon I'll be an old maid."

"You won't be an old maid," her mother replied. "I've heard how wild all of the young men are who have come back from fighting Hitler. They only have one thing on their mind, and my daughter is not going to attend one of those dances."

"But, Mother, where else can I meet young men my age?" Lena asked.

"What about the nice boys at church?" her mother asked.

"They are all too old," Lena said. "Besides, these dances are church sponsored."

"You're not going, Lena, and that's final," her mother said.

Lena could feel the tears starting to roll down her face, when her father, who had remained silent during the whole thing, finally spoke. "Madge, I've heard that the dances are well chaperoned. I think it would be fine for Lena to go."

Lena knew her father seldom crossed her mother on anything, so he must have felt strongly about this. Lena knew her mother understood that as well. Still, her mother didn't like to be challenged.

"Okay," her mother said. Lena was just about to celebrate when her mother continued. "However, I don't want you slipping off to some dark corner." She pulled out a pile of yarn. "To make sure you don't, you can take this and knit a baby blanket so you are not frittering around. And I expect to see it completed."

"But it would take the whole evening to knit even a small blanket," Lena complained, "and I wouldn't get to dance."

"Take it or leave it," her mother said. "Besides, I'm just trying to help you out, since I know you will need one for each of your children when you get married."

Lena felt angry knowing that it was just an excuse, but she nodded and took the knitting and headed out the door. She walked quickly to the church. The dance was already underway when she arrived. There were lots of good-looking guys there, but she found a seat on the side and started to knit. She knitted as fast as she could, hoping to finish and have a chance to dance. Instead, the night was fleeing away and she knew she would never finish in time. An especially good looking guy came in and immediately came and asked her to dance, but she reluctantly turned him down, explaining her situation. As he walked away, she couldn't keep from crying, positive he would never come back.

She had just decided to give up and head home when a group of kindly older women, the chaperones, came back with the young man beside them. Mrs. James held out her hand. "We're really good at knitting."

Lena's tears turned to gratitude as she handed over the knitting and accepted the young man's request to dance. His name was Tom, and she danced the last six dances with him. He offered to walk her home, but she explained that her mother wouldn't approve.

When she arrived home, her mother looked at the completed baby blanket and nodded, but said nothing. Each week after that, Lena met Tom at the dance, and each week she brought home a nice baby blanket.

After some time, Tom came to visit her family. He and her father were instant friends, but it took her mother longer, though Tom's gracious manner eventually won her over, too.

At their wedding reception, the 22 blankets were proudly displayed. Lena's mother wanted to keep some of them, and frowned when Lena's father sternly reminded her that she had promised them to Lena. But Lena had one more surprise coming. After the wedding, Tom pulled her into his arms. "I'm glad your father sent me to meet you at that first dance and explain things to Mrs. James."

Lena gasped and turned to her father. He smiled, nodded, and kissed her cheek.

"But, Lena," he said, "I do agree with Mrs. James that 22 children might be just a few too many."

It Has Been A Long Time

It has been a long time since we've had a baby in our home, and I have almost forgotten what it was like. Our youngest is ten and growing fast. Every once in a while she will still climb up on my lap requesting I read her a story, but, most of the time she reads them herself, and sometimes she even reads them to me.

I have missed having a little one that I can cuddle in my arms and feed a bottle to. I miss having them fall asleep and tucking them into bed.

So, when a young, single mother that we know posted on Facebook that she really needed some help watching her baby, my wife called me to talk about it.

"The mother is going to school and is sick right now," my wife told me. "She could really use someone to take care of her baby for a couple of days while she gets better."

"Sure," I said. "I'd love to have a baby in our home again."

The young mother lives a distance away, so we went to meet her halfway. We arrived at the appointed place, and she came shortly thereafter. She thanked us profusely, saying she was looking forward to getting some much needed rest.

We switched the baby's car seat to our car and buckled the baby in. We were strangers to the baby, and she looked at us with wonderment, but she didn't fuss.

As we traveled she made sweet little baby sounds as my wife played with her. Once we arrived at our home, everyone wanted to hold her. A person pretty much had to take a number for a turn.

Meanwhile, I hunted through our storage to find an old baby bed and other baby things we had put away in case we had a chance to take care of our grandchildren. My wife washed and disinfected all of them so we would be ready for bed time.

I didn't get much chance to hold the baby until evening when our own children went to bed. I changed the baby, dressed her in her pajamas, and sat down to feed her a bottle. She curled up in my arms, and ate as I sang lullabies to her. By the time the last of the formula was draining from the bottle, she was dropping off to dreamland, snuggled up against me.

I spent a little more time just rocking her as she slept, not wanting to hurry the moment too quickly, but, eventually, my wife and I needed to go to bed, too.

I took the sweet little baby and tucked her into the small bed at the foot of ours, wrapping her blanket around her to keep her warm. As I did, she opened one sleepy eye, then drifted back to sleep.

My wife had been fighting a nasty cold the last few nights and had gotten very little sleep, so I volunteered to be the one to get up with the baby in the middle of the night if she cried.

We drifted off to sleep, and it wasn't too long before an unfamiliar sound filled the night. In a daze, I reached up and hit the snooze button on the alarm. A few seconds passed in silence, and then the sound came again. Once more I reached up and not so gently hit the snooze button on the alarm. The sound stopped for a couple of seconds, and then sounded again. Once more I hit the snooze button, but, this time, the sound continued. I started hitting the time set switch, the alarm set, the light button, and basically every button on the clock.

That was when my wife firmly patted me. "It's not the alarm," she said. "It's the baby."

"Baby?" I questioned. My mind started to clear, and I finally put it all together. "Oh, the baby."

I guess it has been a long time since we have had a baby in our house.

An Upset Student And A Letter

It was the end of the semester, and, as usual, I received emails from upset students. Most often the angry emails come from students who are failing because they have not completed their work. Some may have been doing okay through most of the semester, but then, for some reason, they quit coming to class the last few weeks. They also quit taking the exams and doing the homework. The reasons they give are varied, but the effect on their grade is always the same. Then, at the end, they write, wanting to redo the missed material.

This year I received one of the harshest letters I have ever received.

"Dear Professor, I want you to know that I feel your class is the worst class I have ever taken. The material that you expect us to learn is absolutely ridiculous. Not only will I never use it in my life, but it will just take up brain space for stuff that I will use.

"I had heard from other students that this was an easy class and that you were an easy teacher, and that's why I took it. It's not the first class I have taken in this, either. I have also taken similar ones in high school. There, I was always able to finish the work before the end of each class period. I never had any homework. With my background, I should have been able to work through this class easily. But, instead, this class has had tons of stupid new things. I have had up to an hour of homework after every class - way too much. You act like your class is the only thing a person has to do with their life.

"Even with the crazy amount of work that you require, I was still mostly keeping up until a few weeks ago. All of you teachers think your class work is the only thing we have to do. Due to the ridiculous amount of work that other teachers also required, I had fallen behind in those classes and decided I needed to take the time to do them. Because of that, I was not able to come to your class, nor do any of the work. Now that I have caught up in those classes, I logged in to yours, and the assignments won't let me in, saying that they are past due.

"This is stupid. You are without a doubt one of the worst teachers I have ever had. As long as I get the work done, it really shouldn't matter when I do it. You need to open those assignments back up for me."

At this point I quit reading. Though I try to be reasonable, I must admit that I was feeling less than accommodating in this situation. I needed to calm myself. I read some other emails and did some other work. However, I try to always answer every student's email as soon as I can. So, once I felt calmer, I took a deep breath, and went back to reading the letter.

"If you don't let me do those assignments, I plan to go to your department chairman and tell him how unreasonable you are."

At that point, I paused again. My department has a chairwoman, not a chairman. I continued reading.

"Then, instead of teaching basic history classes that poor, unsuspecting new students have to take, they will make you teach some advanced class that nobody even cares about."

I smiled. I have never taught history. I finished the rest of the letter, which was much of the same, and then replied. "I think you probably have the wrong teacher, since I teach math, not history, and you are not on the roll for any of my classes."

The reply came back. "Ha, ha. Yes, silly me. I realized it and tried to recall the email, but couldn't. Funny, huh?"

I smiled and thought, "Yes, but not for you."

The Right Character For The Role

My wife, Donna, and I were directing the musical, **Coming Home**, and we were only a few weeks away from opening night when a lady playing one of the lead roles called us. "I'm sorry," she said, "but I'm going to have to pull out of the production. My mother just had a stroke, and I need to leave town to be with her."

She apologized about leaving us in a tight spot, but we understood. The situation with her mother had to come first. Donna spent two days calling every person we could think of, people who had been in plays and musicals with us before, but she had no luck. Everyone was already involved in something else. Cast members and friends suggested others, but none of them worked out, either.

Donna and I talked about what we should do. "I have a television reporter that is coming tonight to work up a news spot about us," I said. "If we don't have someone to play that part, I don't know how we can do a taping tonight, let alone open in a couple of weeks."

"We have been in tight spots before," Donna replied, "and it has always worked out."

"Yes, but maybe I should cancel having the reporter come," I said. "The scene of the musical we hoped to have on the news is very dependent on the character's part that we can't fill."

"That is true," Donna said, "but we can do another scene if we need to."

The cast came as scheduled, and we started practice. The reporter was a little late, which gave us time to be fully into rehearsal mode before she arrived. When she and her cameraman walked in, I went to greet them.

I held out my hand to her. "You must be Jenny."

She shook my hand, and then she glanced around. "Wow! This is a wonderful old theater."

I nodded. "Yes. It has a lot of character. In fact, like many old theaters, it has its own ghost stories and all sorts of things."

She smiled. "I'm so glad that I was assigned to do this spot. I love theatre, and have always wanted to be in a musical, but I never seem to know when tryouts are. By the time I hear about anything, the rehearsals are always well underway."

"It does take a lot of time to get something like this off the ground," I said, "so tryouts do need to be way ahead of time."

She pulled out some paper and a pencil. "Okay then, let's start with that. How long before opening night do you hold tryouts and start practices?"

Suddenly, seeing her standing there with her paper and pencil sparked a thought. It was so immediate and obvious that I laughed as I spoke. "Actually, we need you to audition tonight."

She looked at me with such a shocked look that her cameraman laughed at her as he spoke to me. "I wished I had had my camera on her when you said that."

I then explained our situation to them. "You see, we had a lady who had to quit because her mother had a stroke, and we need someone to fill her part."

Jenny's eyes danced with excitement. "I'd love to! Do you think I would fit the part?"

"Sure," I answered. "You'd be a natural for it."

We had her practice the lines a few times, and then she performed with us. We even taped it, the very segment we had planned for the television spot originally, and it was perfect. Jenny had fun doing it, and the cameraman had fun filming it.

When we finished, everyone praised Jenny, and she just beamed as she looked forward to her new role. One of the other actors said, "And a star is born. You are so natural for this part."

And of course, she really was, because the character she played happened to be that of the town reporter.

A Little Girl Who Needed An Angel

When I lived in New York, my main mode of transportation was a bike. I worked six days each week, and my bicycle thought that the one day I had free should be spent fixing it. That was what I was doing the day Emily first showed up. I was in the driveway repairing my bike when I heard her voice behind me.

"What the *#&@ are you doing?"

Although I had heard some rough women speak with that kind of language, I had mostly only heard it from men. But when I turned around, to my surprise, I found myself looking into the face of a skinny, little six-year-old girl. Her dark brown hair hung loosely, uncombed, and ragged around her face. Her big brown eyes stared at me questioningly. It took me an instant to regain my composure after realizing it was such a young girl speaking that way.

"I'm fixing my bike," I replied.

"Don't you have any *#&@ thing better to do?" she asked. "I see you working on that *#&@ thing every week."

I laughed, partly at her brazen attitude, partly at her misplaced use of certain profane words, and partly because she was right about how much I worked on it.

"It does seem to need a lot of work, doesn't it?" I agreed.

"Why don't you get a new one?" she asked.

"I can't afford it," I replied.

"I know a guy that will steal whatever *#&@ bike you want for only ten bucks," she said. "Do you want me to talk to him for you?"

"Well, that's, uh, nice of you," I replied, not knowing if that was quite the correct response, "but I think I will just keep this one."

"Your loss."

She stared at me curiously and intently, and it made me feel somewhat uncomfortable, so I turned back to work on my bike as I talked. "So, what's your name?"

"Emily."

"Where do you live?" I asked.

"423 Elm Street."

I had to stifle my surprise. Elm Street was miles away through a really rough part of the city.

"What brings you over here?" I asked.

"To be away from home," she replied. "Last Friday, school got out for the summer, and today my step-dad told me to get out of the house, because he was 'sick of seeing my *#&@ ugly face.'"

In an instant, I knew much about this little girl. I had come across many children like her before. Knowing how far away she lived, I asked, "Aren't you concerned about getting home for lunch?"

"I'm not allowed home until dark," she replied.

My heart ached for her as I considered what her home life must be like. "Would you like to eat lunch with me?" I asked. "It won't be anything fancy, just peanut butter and jelly sandwiches."

She nodded vigorously, and I led her into the house. My landlady was there, and I introduced Emily to her. "I'm *#&@ glad to meet you," Emily said.

My landlady, a very proper Polish woman, raised her eyebrows slightly at such language. Emily ate nearly a loaf of my homemade bread, each slice smothered in strawberry jam. She also drank two full glasses of milk.

As she finished, she asked, "Are you an angel?"

"What do you mean?" I asked in surprise.

"Someone told me that God has people that are called angels, and they work for Him and help someone that needs help. I thought you might be one of them, and I was really hungry, so that's why I came here."

I smiled at her. "Well, Emily, I suppose that, sometimes, God can have common people be angels to help someone." I thought about that, and then added, "And if you are ever hungry, or need somewhere to go, you come on over."

And, though I know I'm no angel, I wondered if God had brought Emily to me.

A Bicycle For A Little Girl

Six-year-old Emily showed up at our house because she was hungry and didn't know where else to go. Her step father had told her to always be out of the house before daylight and to never come home before dark. From then on, through that summer, she showed up for breakfast by 6:30, and was waiting when Henton, the young man I worked with, and I came home for lunch or dinner. I always made lots of food so she would have plenty.

I was 20 years old, and Emily became like a little sister. On my days off she would help me work on my bicycle. She learned the names of each wrench in my small tool set, and would happily hand them to me when I asked.

One morning she came dragging a little bicycle into the driveway. "A friend of mine found this bike and said I could have it," she said. "Can you help me fix it?"

I knew that more likely her friend had stolen it, and, finding it didn't work, knew he couldn't sell it. It was kind of an ugly bike, with some painted bears on it, but, to Emily, it was the most beautiful bike in the world.

I checked it out. "Emily," I said, "this bike is going to need two new tubes, one new tire tread, and some new pedals." I walked to the other side, "It looks like it could use a new seat, and . . . "

I stopped as I caught sight of Emily and saw tears forming in her eyes. "It would cost too *#&@ much to fix, huh?" she asked.

I looked at this sweet, rough little girl. She had little to look forward to in life. I couldn't be the one to disappoint her.

"You really like this bike, don't you?" I asked.

She nodded. "Well, I suppose it wouldn't cost that much," I lied. "It will just take some time."

Her tears turned to a smile as she talked about how exciting it would be to have her own bike. Henton and I took her with us, and I carried the bike to a little bike shop. When Mr. Johnson, the store owner, priced all the parts I would need, I knew it was going to really be hard on my budget. Feeding Emily had more than doubled my food bill.

"I can buy half of them now, and the other half next month," I told him. "Which ones are most important?"

Mr. Johnson, who was old enough to be Emily's grandfather, paused and looked at her. "Aren't you the little girl who is always in here looking at bikes?" Emily nodded. "Is this going to be your bike?" Again she nodded. He smiled and turned to me, "You know, the shop ain't that busy right now. You just pay for half of them, I'll donate the other half, and I'll fix it up for free."

I nodded my agreement, and Emily ran to him and gave him a big hug. The old man smiled. "I'd say a hug is darned good pay."

I paid my part, and, a few days later, we took Emily to the store to pick up her bike. Her happiness was pay enough for all of us. As we left the store, Emily turned to me. "Is Mr. Johnson one of the angels you told me about that God has here that helps people?"

I nodded. "I'm sure he is, Emily. There are lots of them all around us."

Emily rode her bike everywhere after that, and everyone loved her and watched out for her. One Saturday, as she ate dinner with us, she was unusually quiet. "What's the matter, Emily?" I asked.

"You go to church every Sunday and learn about God, don't you?" she asked. I nodded, so she continued. "Do you think God would let me come to church, too?"

"Of course He would," I said. "Why do you ask?"

"Because I want to become an angel and help people, too," she replied

"You don't have to go to church to be an angel or to help people," I said.

"Well, I still want to go," she said, "because I want to be a proper angel."

I turned to Henton. "I think it's time we go to 423 Elm Street and have a visit with Emily's step dad."

Dogged Every Step Of The Way

Six-year-old Emily showed up at our house because she was hungry, and she didn't know where else to go. Her step father had told her to always be out of the house before daylight, and to never come home until after dark. I started feeding her every day, and she became a wonderful part of our lives. But when she asked me if she could go to church with us, I knew it was time to visit her home.

I worked with a young man named Henton, and he and I made our way over to Elm. We turned and headed down the street, looking for 423. The further we went, the rougher the neighborhood grew. We looked out of place in our suits, and the few people we passed on the street stopped to stare at us. When we stopped at 423, an interesting sight met our eyes.

The grass was about a foot tall, probably never having been mowed all summer. Beer cans littered the walk and front porch. There was trash everywhere. An old broken couch with stuffing coming out of it sat under an old tree.

As soon as we stopped, two large dogs came running toward us, snarling and growling. Henton jumped behind me. The dogs stopped at the edge of the property, daring us to come any further.

I turned to Henton. "You ready for this?"

He shook his head. "If you're going to the door, you're going alone."

I was determined to get the needed permission, so I steeled myself, took my umbrella in my right hand to defend myself, if necessary, and stepped forward. The dogs jumped toward me, but, as I moved my umbrella threateningly, they backed off. As I made my way to the door, they circled me. When they would act like they were going to lunge, I'd move my umbrella toward them, and they would retreat.

I finally made it to the porch. The dogs stayed on the steps, snarling. I kept an eye on them while I knocked on the door. When the door opened, there stood a fat, slovenly man, dressed in ragged shorts, no shirt, and holding a beer in his hand. He looked at me standing there, glanced at Henton on the street, and spoke with a quivering voice.

"Hey, look. I don't want no *#&@ trouble. Tell Dexter I'll get him the money. He's got my word."

"I don't know any Dexter," I said.

He sized me up for a moment, and then spoke again. "You're a cop, ain't you? Look, you ain't got nothing on me. Not a *#&@ thing."

"I'm not a cop," I said. "I'm a friend of Emily's."

"Oh, I see," he said. "Well, we take good care of her. We don't need no Family Services check."

"I'm not with Family Services," I replied.

"Well, who the *#&@ are you, then?" he asked.

"I'm just Emily's friend," I replied. "She asked if she could go to church with us, and I wanted to get your permission."

He looked like he had been hit by a truck. "You came all the way here, past my dogs, to ask me if Emily can go to church with you?"

"Yes, sir," I replied.

"Sir?" he choked. "Well, don't that beat all? Ain't no one ever called me that before. Sure, you can take Emily with you, as long as she stays out of trouble, and no one comes here a preachin'."

"Would you mind signing a permission slip?" I asked.

He shrugged. He couldn't find any paper, so he unfolded a cigarette carton and signed his name below the words "Emily can go to church."

As I stuffed the cigarette carton into my pocket and headed out the door, he yelled at the dogs to leave me alone. With one final growl they slunk away.

He laughed. "Either you are the *#&@ bravest man I've ever seen, or you are the *#&@ stupidest. I can't believe my dogs didn't tear you to pieces."

"Emily says she thinks I am one of God's angels sent to help her," I said.

"So what does that have to do with them not biting you?" he asked.

"Maybe your dogs decided it's not a good idea to bite an angel," I replied.

A First Time At Church

Six-year-old Emily showed up at our house because she was hungry. She became a wonderful part of our lives, and when she asked me if she could go to church with us, I braved my way past her stepdad's dogs to get permission.

But now came the hard part - getting Emily ready for church. I knew I needed help in this endeavor, so I approached our old Polish landlady, Mrs. Salak, about it. She was a very proper woman, and her eyebrows always rose when she heard Emily's swearing. So, when I asked Mrs. Salak if she'd help, her ready agreement to do so caught me by surprise.

"I would love to take on that challenge," she said.

She searched through the dresses from her own daughter's youth, and found one, probably from the 50's. It was a beautiful flower print. Emily began to question whether she wanted to go through with this when Mrs. Salak announced it was bath time. Emily probably hadn't bathed more than once in any given month, and, from her hollering and swearing, I was sure she was getting a first rate scrubbing. But that paled in comparison to the brushing of her knotted hair.

"My heavens, Emily, how often do you brush your hair?" Mrs. Salak asked.

"Ain't never had need of one of those *#&@ things," Emily replied.

They were both stubborn, and though Mrs. Salak was firm, and Emily complained, I sensed that Mrs. Salak enjoyed the progress, and Emily enjoyed the attention. I left them to their task and finished my work. An hour or so before church was to start, Mrs. Salak invited me in to see the transformation.

And what a transformation it was! Instead of a little girl with long, knotted hair, wearing worn out blue jeans and a t-shirt, there stood a beautiful young lady. I moved Emily to a mirror and stood behind her.

"So, what do you think, Emily?" I asked.

"I think I look *#&@ stupid," she replied.

"Well, I think you look like a beautiful young lady," I said. She beamed at the compliment, as did Mrs. Salak.

My colleague, Henton, and I had an early meeting at the church. We were waiting in the foyer when Mrs. Salak and Emily walked in. The leader of the congregation, whom we called "The Bishop", came over to meet Emily.

Emily shook his hand. "I'm *#&@ glad to meet you," she said.

The Bishop smiled and welcomed her. Emily then turned to me. "So when do I get to meet God?"

"Well, you don't actually ever see Him here," I replied.

"Why?" she asked. "Is He off to a meeting, or helping someone like you always are?"

I laughed. "Something like that." But I knew I had a lot of teaching to do.

Emily sat with us through part of church, then she went to the children's classes. I had her meet the lady in charge of those classes, Mrs. Stanton, and Emily shook her hand.

"It is nice to have you here, Emily," Mrs. Stanton said.

"Thank you," Emily said. "It's *#&@ nice to be here."

Mrs. Stanton smiled and glanced at me, and I knew it was past time for me to visit with Emily about her language. I knew it even more so after church when Mrs. Stanton kindly, but firmly, mentioned that the other children were repeating what Emily said.

Later, when I mentioned to Emily that it would be best if she didn't use certain words, she looked surprised and asked why.

"Because our words reflect the kind of person we are," I replied. "And a beautiful young lady doesn't speak that way."

Emily agreed to do her best not to swear, and then she asked, "When can I find out if God will let me be one of his angels to help other people like you do?"

"He has called everyone to be one," I told her. "A person just has to find out how and where."

"So why do you go to church," she asked, "to be better than other people?"

"No," I replied. "Going to church doesn't help a person be better than someone else; it only helps them be better than they themselves currently are."

Emily smiled. "Then I hope I can keep going to church forever."

Angels Covered In Tattoos And Dressed In Leather

Six-year-old Emily showed up at our house because her stepfather didn't allow her to come home during the day, and she was hungry. Since then, she had become a wonderful part of my life. But, as time went on, I knew I would soon finish my work in the area and would be transferred. I was concerned about Emily. Who would watch out for her? Then my answer came.

One day my colleague and I were out working. Upon walking into a neighborhood, we heard a girl scream. I knew it was Emily, and looked toward the end of the street. A young man was trying to take her bike from her, and she was hanging on to it.

I dropped the things I was carrying and ran toward the two of them. Before I could get there, they were suddenly surrounded by a group of rough looking young men who were covered in tattoos and dressed in leather. I didn't know what I could do against all of them, but, fearing for her safety, I never even slowed.

As I approached the group, Emily saw me and ran to me, throwing herself into my arms. However, the situation was far different than I had thought, for the leader of the group of young men was speaking harshly to the man who had been trying to take the bike. "What are you doing to Emily?"

"This happens to be my bike," he replied bravely. "I'd recognize it anywhere."

"Oh, you'd look cute riding a bike with Teddy Bears on it," one of the young men said.

The group laughed, but the first young man stood his ground. "I meant it was my little sister's bike."

"That's a lie," the group leader said. "I found this bike when it was just a piece of junk, and I gave it to Emily. She's the one that got it fixed up."

"It still belonged to my sister," the first one said, "and she should get something for it."

Feeling out of place in my suit, I stepped into the circle, and everyone turned to stare at me. "How much do you think your sister should have for it?" I asked.

"Ten bucks," he replied.

"Ten bucks!" the group leader said. "*#&@, it weren't worth a dime."

I dug into my wallet, pulled out eight ones and awkwardly fumbled for enough change to make the other two dollars. Finally, when I had enough, I handed it to him. "Here's the money. Now, you leave Emily alone."

As the young man was about to leave, the group leader grabbed him by the shirt. "If you ever touch Emily again, it will be the last conscious thing you ever do. Got it?"

The young man nodded. The group leader then gave the young man a shove toward the street, and he headed off as fast as he could run. The group leader then turned to me. "I see you're a friend of Emily's."

I nodded. "And I see you are, too."

"We all are," one of the other men said.

"And no one better touch Emily while we're around," another one added. "Or they will be *#&@ sorry."

The leader held out his hand to do a knuckle bump. "J.C.'s the name, but most people call me Astro."

I introduced myself, and each of the young men in turn introduced themselves, with each introduction followed by a knuckle bump.

"Thanks for helping Emily," I said.

"You, too," the leader replied.

They all wandered off, leaving Emily alone with me.

"Emily, you know how you asked if God provides angels to watch over you?" I asked.

"Yes," she replied.

"Well, it looks like sometimes those angels come covered in tattoos and dressed in leather," I said.

Six-year-old Emily showed up at our house because she was hungry, and her stepfather didn't allow her to come home during the day. After that, she became a wonderful part of my life. But, when I knew my transfer day was coming, I became concerned about who would watch out for her. I quickly realized, however, that there were many who would do so.

As fall came, and Emily started back to school, she continued to ride her bike to our house for breakfast, and returned after school for dinner. Her school was close to where we lived, so it worked out well. Each morning, my landlady, Mrs. Salak, made sure that Emily had on neat, clean clothes, and that her hair was brushed. Emily had mostly quit swearing, but she hated having her hair brushed, and swore a bit then. With all of the care Mrs. Salak gave her, Emily started fitting in better at school. She didn't get teased as much, and ended up fighting less, coming to dinner with fewer bruises.

When my transfer notice came, I knelt in front of her and started to explain that I was going to be leaving. I hadn't even finished before she burst into tears and threw her arms around my neck, holding me so tightly I could hardly breathe as she cried, "No, no, no, no!"

When she finally calmed down, I had her look at me, and then explained that she now had lots of friends to watch over her. Mrs. Salak told Emily that she wanted her to continue coming over, and that she would feed and take care of her as I had.

When I was transferred, it was hard to say goodbye. I wish I could say Emily's life was perfect after that, but nothing works that way. The abuse Emily received from her stepfather became worse, and the state threatened to take her away. That was when her mother came to visit Mrs. Salak. Rather than lose her daughter into state custody, they worked it out for Emily to live with Mrs. Salak, where Emily's mother could come visit.

From then on, Emily was raised mostly by Mrs. Salak and the kind people of the church and community. Mrs. Salak was in her 70's by then, and it was challenging for her to take care of an obstinate little girl. And when Emily reached her teens, the challenge became greater still. But it was Mrs. Salak's values that Emily grew to emulate - values of honesty, thrift, hard work, and virtue.

In return, it was Mrs. Salak who was there to see Emily go to her first prom. It was Mrs. Salak who proudly stood with Emily in her high school graduation pictures. And it was Mrs. Salak who held the place of honor as Emily's mother at Emily's wedding when Emily married a wonderful young man she met at church.

Mrs. Salak was old by then, in her late 80's. She never had a lot of money, but what she did have she usually spent on Emily. The members of the church all pooled resources for a beautiful reception, and Mrs. Salak even had a new dress, probably the only one she had ever had in all the years she was raising Emily.

After the wedding, Emily had a new family to love her - her husband's - and she grew to love them, too. Mrs. Salak only lived a few more years after the wedding, but it was long enough for her to be able to hold Emily's first child, a girl, whom they lovingly named Lavinia. Lavinia was Mrs. Salak's first name, and she was proud of her namesake, loving her as if she were her own granddaughter, for in reality, she truly was.

It has been many years since then. Lavinia is now a beautiful young lady, and has other siblings. Sometimes it is hard for me to believe that Emily was that swearing little six-year-old girl that sought me out because she thought I was one of the angels someone had told her were sent to help people. But, through her, I learned that there truly are angels all around us.

And to me, Mrs. Salak and Emily definitely were two of them.

I was only five years old, and didn't attend kindergarten. Life can be quite boring when a person has to play all alone. But school break had just started, and my brothers and sisters were home for the summer. Life was just about to become more exciting.

Fathers' Day was not long after summer break started, and I was trying to figure out something I could do for my father. I didn't have any money, so buying a gift was out of the question. That was when my brother, Albert, came to me and said he had a great idea; something we could do that would be a wonderful gift for Dad.

"You know how the garbage has piled up in the garage, and no one has been able to haul it away because they are all busy planting crops?" he asked. I nodded, so he continued. "We'll take it out to the field on the edge of the desert and burn it."

I knew that Albert had had a great fascination with fire recently, and that almost every idea he had come up with since school let out had involved matches, but I had to admit that it sounded like a great gift.

"You bag up the garbage and get it in your wagon," he said. "I will get the other necessary items."

We didn't have any nice garbage bags back then, so I found some old gunny sacks and stuffed the garbage into them. The garbage filled four sacks as tightly as I could pack them. I laid them in a pile crosswise on the wagon. I had just finished when Albert showed up. He indicated he was ready by patting the matches in his bulging pocket.

It was about a half mile to the field where we were headed. It was on the north side of our farm next to open range land that was covered with dry grasses and sage brush. On our way there we stopped at a pile of wood. Albert pulled out a gallon of something that he had hidden away.

"What's that?" I asked.

"Oh, just a little gasoline," he replied, as nonchalantly as if it was drinking water for a long trip.

We continued on our way and soon arrived at our destination. The field was about 50 acres, so we had a nice, wide-open space. We dumped out the bags into a big pile. Albert poured a generous amount of gasoline on it and then pulled a match from his pocket.

"All right," he said with a grin, "Here we go."

Finding a rock, he swiped the match across it. It immediately burst into a blue and red flame. He then tossed the match toward the pile of garbage.

Since my curiosity was greater than my common sense, I was standing much closer to the pile of garbage than I should have been. Immediately the garbage and everything near it burst into flames, and my eyebrows and the front part of my hair disappeared. As the garbage burned, pieces of it floated into the air for a short distance before dropping into the dry grass. The grass instantly caught fire.

"Quick!" Albert yelled. "Stomp out the fires!"

We ran from fire to fire stomping. And, although it got ahead of us at times, the main fire began to burn itself out, and we finally started to win. By the time everything seemed to be totally under control, we were exhausted. It was all I could do to drag my little red wagon back to the house.

Albert was unusually kind, saying, "Why don't you wash, and I'll get you some lunch." I didn't realize he wasn't concerned about me, but about having others see me missing my hair and eyebrows. I ate what he brought to me and dropped into bed for a nap.

But the excitement wasn't over yet. I was barely asleep when the fire engines' sirens woke me as they roared past our house.

You see, our gift was one of those kinds that was going to just keep on giving.

An Exciting Summer Day

When I was only five years old, my older brother, Albert, talked me into helping him burn the garbage that had been collecting in our garage. He said that it would be a great Fathers' Day gift. We had taken it to the field on the north of our farm, right on the edge of the desert. All went okay, except for the fact that I lost my eyebrows and the front of my hair from standing too close to the fire.

We had come back from our little adventure, and, being very tired, I took a nap. I had barely fallen asleep when the roar of fire engine sirens woke me. I rubbed the sleep from my eyes and went outside to join my brothers and sisters. More fire engines roared by, and I looked to the north and could see grey smoke billowing into the sky.

"Hey," Daniel said. "Let's climb up into the barn so we can see what's happening."

Everyone agreed, so we made our way there. Our barn was one of those tall ones from a previous era that was the height of a four-story building. We all climbed into the loft and then climbed the ladder to the opening at the back. My brothers and sisters all sat on the opening ledge, but, since I was the youngest, I was not allowed to do something so dangerous, and had to stand on the ladder to look out.

Beyond our farm, to the north, lay miles and miles of range land covered with dry grass and sagebrush. This was what was on fire. Luckily, it was an unusually windless day, and the fire was moving slowly.

We watched as truck after truck emptied their loads along the fire line, and then rushed back to the ditch by our house to fill their tanks with more water. The brave firefighters were gradually encircling the fire rim, but, despite their best efforts, they could not stop the fire from reaching the power line that ran across the open range.

We watched as the first power pole started to tip. Soon, others near it began to lean, and then, suddenly, a whole section of the line crashed to the ground. As the poles hit the ground, they sparked a new round of fires, and the firemen raced to head them off.

The battle continued all day, but, as the sun started to approach the horizon, the firemen finished and started to wind up their hoses. The blackened land stretched out in a visible V shape.

"Look at that," John said. "It looks like the fire started at a point in our north pasture."

"Not only that," I chimed in, trying to be helpful, "Albert and I are very lucky that it didn't start until after we finished burning the garbage there, or we could have been hurt."

Everyone turned and looked at me, and, with my missing eyebrows and missing hair, they just assumed they knew the whole story and that I was guilty.

"You and Albert burned garbage out there?" John asked.

Albert had told me about the Fifth Amendment, and I figured it was time to invoke my rights and not incriminate myself anymore. When everyone turned to where Albert had been, he was gone. I barely remembered that, in the excitement, he had slipped past me, heading down the ladder.

"Where did Albert go?" Daniel asked. I just shrugged.

Until hunger drove Albert from his hiding place, he was impossible to find. That left me alone to face my parents. My father, who had helped fight the fire, was tired, covered in soot, and unhappy.

My punishment was severe. I was to spend weeks working at Grandma's house, where she could keep an eye on me so I couldn't get into more trouble. For hours on end I had to dig grass, and every other miserable weed known to man, from her garden. It was hot and boring.

Well, I should say that it was boring until the day I

discovered what a person could do with Grandma's magnifying glass on a hot day.

And thank heavens for that Fifth Amendment, which meant I didn't have to explain how her garden shed randomly caught on fire.

How To Get Pizza For Free

It was district scout night, and all of the troop leaders met together at 6:00 P.M. for training. "There is nothing more important than making sure the boys are well fed," the district leader said, as he started the meeting. "A full boy is a happy boy."

He then proceeded to give us a PowerPoint presentation. It consisted of 25 plan-ahead recipes. The first one was fajitas with big chunks of chicken and vegetables wrapped in soft taco shells and smothered in chunky tomato salsa. The second food was scones. The pictures showed them nice and brown, dripping with butter, and then smothered in either honey or raspberry jam.

I hadn't had a chance to eat dinner before I came, and my stomach grumbled as I looked at the pictures of the food. The district leader took 30 minutes going through his PowerPoint, and, by the time he finished, my hunting instinct made me want to kill and eat a sandwich. But we still had another 30 minutes of group meetings. I joined the other five scoutmasters, while the six men who worked with the varsity scouts met in the room next to us.

Jack, the man in charge of our group, called the meeting to order. "We will be going over knots tonight."

A big burly man named Devin complained. "Knots? How in the world do you expect us to think about knots with our stomachs grumbling from that show about food?"

"There will be cookies and punch after the meeting," Jack replied.

"Cookies and punch after seeing fajitas and scones?" Devin asked. "I don't think so. I need real food, like pizza."

"Well," Jack said. "I suppose we could order some pizza to be delivered while we work on our knots. Everybody want to donate?"

We checked among our group, but we only had two dollars between the six of us, and we knew that the delivery person couldn't take a check. "Well I guess we're out of luck," Jack said.

"Not so fast," Devin replied. "I know the man in charge of the Varsity Scout group, and believe me, Ron always carries money."

Devin pulled out his cell phone and started to dial.

"Who are you calling?" Jack asked.

"The pizza place," Devin replied.

"But we don't have enough money," Jack said.

Devin laughed. "I'll show you how to get pizza for free."

The pizza place answered, and Devin spoke into his phone. "I would like to order some pizzas." He paused, listening, and then spoke again. "I don't know. Hang on a minute." He turned to us. "There are six of them in the next room, right?" We nodded, so he turned back to the phone. "There are 12 of us, so how many pizzas would you suggest?"

He ended up ordering six pizzas, far more than suggested, and, as he was ending, he said, "Oh, and the name on it will be Ron." He then gave the next door room number for the delivery.

We started tying knots, but the minute we heard the pizza delivery guy at the room next door, Devin led us down there. He stopped us just before the door, and we watched and waited as the six men inside tried to figure out where the pizzas had come from, and then pooled their money together to pay for it.

They had no sooner paid the bill, and the pizza delivery man had left, than Devin stuck his head in the door. "Did you guys order pizza?"

"It's crazy," Ron said. "We were all sitting here wishing we had some, and then this pizza guy just shows up. It was like he knew or something."

"Are you going to eat all six of those?" Devin asked.

102

Ron shook his head. "There's no way. Why don't you guys join us?"

"And that," Devin whispered to us as we joined them, "is how you get free pizza."

After all, a full scoutmaster is a happy scoutmaster.

When Something Gets Your Goat

I really love mountain goats. I think they are incredible animals. One of my main hopes on our vacation last year to Glacier National Park was to be able to take a picture of one of these elusive creatures, with a majestic mountain in the background.

On our first day of vacation, we drove all day to get there and arrived late in the evening. We set up camp and I prepared dinner. I cooked Dutch oven potatoes and steak, and finished off with Dutch oven cobbler. We didn't stay up too late that night, wanting to be on our way as early as possible to some hiking trails.

The sun was barely coming up when I climbed out of bed and started breakfast. I cooked bacon and pancakes so we would have a hearty meal to sustain us through a long day. The aroma of the cooking bacon brought the children sleepily out of their beds.

When we finished eating, we quickly cleaned up. We walked to the bus stop, and, as we stood there, we suddenly remembered that we had forgotten our camera. I ran the half mile back to camp, and then ran the return trip as well. I was feeling very oxygen deficient by the time I turned the last corner and saw the bus loading people at the bus stop. I increased my speed, and made it just before the bus pulled out, and just before I passed out.

We rode the park bus up Going-To-The-Sun Road, enjoying the incredible vistas. When we reached Logan Pass, we disembarked and entered the visitors' center to see if there were any reports of mountain goat sightings. We heard of one and headed on our way on that trail.

The trail started out meandering through a meadow, but soon rose steeply up the mountain and then ran for miles along a 200-foot vertical drop. To say that our family has a fear of heights is an understatement. Some of our children began to breathe hard, not from exertion, but from fear. We told them to just keep their eyes on the mountain and to not look down as we pressed on mile after mile. But eventually, everyone was exhausted. In addition, there were complaints of blisters. So we finally decided we could not continue and had to turn back.

We found a small wooded area that hid the view of the steep drop so we could calm our nerves while we ate some lunch. Once we were slightly rested, we started back.

The hike back took even longer, since everyone was tired and sore and we had to rest frequently. Eventually we arrived at the visitors' center. We were disappointed that, in all of our hours of hiking, we had not seen anything except a few squirrels and some chipmunks. We took pictures of them, but we knew they were not the kind of photography that would make the cover of Wild Life Extraordinaire.

While the others sat down to rest, I limped into the gift shop to hunt for a post card of a mountain goat. Even if we weren't able to see one on our hike, we were for sure going to have a picture of one to take home with us.

I finally found a suitable picture, and bought a post card for each member of the family. When I walked out, a bus that could take us back to our campground was just pulling in. As sore, tired, and blistered as we were, we hurried as fast as we could push ourselves so we could make it.

As we came around the front of the bus to climb on, there, not 50 feet from us, stood two mountain goats grazing on the hillside. As we stopped and stared at them, I turned to my wife.

"You know what?" I said. "I really hate mountain goats."

Gordy stormed out of his tent and marched right over to where I was checking ingredients for Dutch oven cobbler. "I knew it!" he hollered. "I thought it was happening, and now I have proof!"

"What?" I asked.

"There is a thief here at scout camp," he replied. "I thought I had things disappearing, and so I set a trap."

"Oh really?" I asked. "What did you catch?"

"I didn't catch nothin' yet, but I'm going to," he replied. "And when I do, somebody is going to find themselves thrown into the icy creek."

"If you didn't catch anyone, then how do you know somebody is stealing stuff?" I asked.

"I counted every one of my Oreo cookies before I headed off to work on my merit badge," he replied, "and I had 22 of them. When I came back, the package only contained 21."

I felt relieved that the total loss was only one Oreo cookie. I had envisioned things to be much worse. "Isn't Mort the one sharing the tent with you?" I asked. "How do you know it wasn't him?"

"Because he was with me at the merit badge station the whole time," Gordy said, eying me suspiciously. "But you were here in camp."

"I was," I admitted. "But I can promise you that I didn't steal your cookie. I was up half the night chasing that bear out of our camp, and so, when I finished with clean up, I took a nap. And I never heard anything."

"How could you, if you were asleep?"

"Good question," I replied. "However, I think sleeping bags are quite misnamed. I can hardly sleep in one."

"Well, I'm going to catch whoever it is," Gordy said.

"Are you sure you didn't just miscount the cookies?" I asked.

"Yes," Gordy replied. "And besides, the package was turned. I laid it out square with my wallet at one corner and my IPod at the other so I could tell if it was moved, and when I came back, it was twisted at an angle."

"Let me get this straight," I said. "You laid out your IPod and your wallet to mark the orientation of the cookie package so you could determine for sure if someone was stealing a ten-cent cookie?"

Gordy nodded enthusiastically. "Pretty smart, huh?"

It was hard, but I held back my smile. "Absolutely genius," I replied.

"And it's not just cookies," Gordy said. "I'm sure I've been losing some of my candy, too. I'm planning on setting a trap for that as well."

"What do you plan to do?" I asked.

"I don't know," he replied. "Do you have any suggestions?"

"Maybe you could turn the volume up on your IPod, and then maybe he'll listen to it when he's eating the candy, and we'll know he's there."

"Ha, ha. Real funny," Gordy said. "Thousands of comedians out of work, and I get stuck with you."

I laughed. "Well, maybe, instead, you could get some of that red paint from the leather working merit badge station and put that on the outside of the candy wrappers."

Gordy became excited at the prospect. "Do you think that will work?"

"Sure," I said. "There is nothing like catching a thief red handed."

Scout camp was going pretty much as usual. Gordy had had an Oreo cookie stolen, and he was sure someone was taking his candy, too. He was determined to find a way to catch the bandit. That was when I suggested that he paint the candy wrappers with red paint acquired from the leather working merit badge station. And that was exactly what he did, just before he left the next morning to work on merit badges.

I was around camp most of the morning and saw nothing unusual, but, when everyone returned for lunch, Gordy's painted candies were missing. He demanded everyone show him their hands, but the only person with any paint on himself was Gordy from his sloppy paint job. He couldn't try this technique again, since everyone now knew what he had done. But it didn't matter to him, because, in his mind, everyone was guilty, and he wasn't reluctant about saying so.

"Okay, Gordy," I said, "calm down, and let's try to analyze this."

"That's stupid," he replied. "Just because you're a math professor doesn't mean you can solve something like this by logic."

"No," I said, "but sometimes the answers are different from what a person may think. And, often, they are right in front of a person's face."

"And if it is Gordy's face," Devin said, "then it could be a really ugly answer."

"Ha, ha," Gordy replied. "Thousands of comedians out of work and I get stuck with you."

"Let's consider some things," I said. "Gordy, did you zip your tent shut when you left?"

"Of course."

"Was it still shut when you came back?"

"Almost," he replied. "The zipper was up about four or five inches."

"Was it the same way last time when you lost the Oreo?"

"Yes."

"If a thief wanted to remain unsuspected," I said, "I'm sure that he would have tried to leave things exactly the same."

"So why only leave it up four to five inches?" Tanner asked.

I thought about it for a minute as the whole troop stared at me, acting like I was going to get some kind of revelation or something. And then, suddenly, I did get one. I smiled as the answer began to come to me. "Maybe it was up only four or five inches because that was all the thief needed," I said.

"That's stupid," Gordy said. "Obviously he couldn't crawl in that hole. And I put the candy at the far back of the tent so he couldn't reach his arm in and grab it."

I smiled, and that seemed to build the suspense and curiosity for everyone. "Gordy, were there any other signs or anything?" I asked.

"Well, the thief dripped a little paint in the tent," Gordy replied.

Everyone followed as I went to look at the evidence. Upon inspection I shook my head. "That's not dripped paint."

"What is it?" Mort asked.

Instead of answering, I scanned the trees. The boys looked up, trying to see what I was looking for. Finally, I saw it. I smiled as I answered them. "It wasn't dripped paint; it was foot prints."

"Foot prints?" Gordy questioned.

I had seen a squirrel often watching us. But now, its paws and whole underbelly were red. I pointed at it. "There's your thief."

Gordy looked up and saw the red paint on the squirrel. He walked over to the tree, and sure enough, the ground was littered with candy wrappers. He shook his fist at it. "You dirty little thief!"

The squirrel shook his fist back and shouted "Chi, chi, chi!"

"You little beggar!" Gordy yelled. He picked up a stick and threw it up at the squirrel. The stick came right back and hit Gordy on his foot. He started jumping around and hollering.

"Squirrel 10, Gordy 0," Devin said.

And, thus, was solved the case of the scout camp bandit.

A Kitten Named Oliver

I had always said I could never be fond of a cat because cats are annoying animals. On our farm, the cats were wild and pesky. To make matters worse, when I married, my mother-in-law owned a cat; or, to be more specific, the cat owned her. It bothered me when the cat demanded it be served like a queen and my mother-in-law indulged its behavior. So, from experience, I felt I would always dislike cats.

Then I met Oliver.

I had gone out to my mother's house to help her with her garden. I was trimming some trees for her when a little yellow kitten came out of a hole near the tree's roots. It was crying, and tried to climb my pant leg. I didn't want to touch it, afraid its mother wouldn't take it back, so I used my foot to push it back into the hole. But no matter how many times I did, it kept coming back. Not only that, but its cry was joined by a whole chorus, and I soon had a whole litter of kittens around my feet. Besides that first yellow one, there were four others of assorted greys and blacks.

I moved away from that tree so their mother would return, but I kept watch from a distance. No mother cat ever came, and, by the end of the day, I realized none ever would. I knew that if I didn't feed them, they would die. So I put them in a box and took them home.

They were so small we had to feed them with a doll bottle. Although they were starving, it was hard to get them to understand how to eat. At least it was for all of them except that first yellow one. He latched onto that bottle and drained it quickly. As much as we tried, we eventually lost the other four, even as the yellow one thrived.

I insisted that I would not be a nursemaid to a kitten, but, when the children started back to school, I was home alone with it, and I couldn't stand to see it go hungry. I would tuck it in the nook of my arm and feed it its bottle like a baby. Soon, it trusted me and didn't want anyone else to feed it.

The family felt I should be the one to name it, so, using all of my creative genius, I declared it would have the name of "Cat". My family was disgusted and wanted me to do better, so I changed the name to Oliver after the orphan in "Oliver Twist".

As Oliver grew, he decided he was my cat. He would follow me like a dog when I went out to do chores. If I ever sat down, he was immediately on my lap. This became quite a feat as he grew.

But the thing that really endeared him to me was his personality. He was not like other cats. The other cats would fight for a position at the food bowl, but he would wait patiently for his share. The only times I ever saw him growl was when we had a new batch of kittens. He would then push the bigger cats away and make them wait until the kittens had eaten first.

Each night, as the air would turn cold, the kittens would leave their mothers and curl up with Oliver instead. He was much bigger than the mother cats and had more fur to keep the kittens warm.

Sometimes, when a mother cat didn't have enough milk for all of her kittens, she would abandon one. When she did, Oliver would bring it to me. He knew from his own experience that we would feed it. Over the years Oliver raised many batches of kittens, more than any mother cat. The only thing he wouldn't do was to lick them clean, but, then, that was the one thing I refused to do for him when I raised him.

Then came the day I came home from work and found out Oliver had died. As I went out to do chores and he wasn't there following me, I sat down on a bale of hay as the hurt in my heart seemed unbearable.

I realized that I had truly learned to love an animal that I never thought I could.

My wife, Donna, sent me to town to purchase the last items we had on our list for our vacation. I was working my way down the bread aisle at Wal-Mart when a lady stopped me.

"I'm sorry to bother you," she said, "but I'm not from around here. Could you tell me what is a good brand of bread?"

We usually make our own bread, but when we do buy some at the store, there are certain varieties I prefer, so I told her which ones they were and why we like them.

"So, where are you from?" I asked when I finished.

She told me, and then I asked her what she thought of our area. "It's beautiful here," she said. "The sky is always blue, and it never rains. Where I am from it rains every day, and often a couple of times per day. Another thing I like is the open space. A person can look out and see for miles." She paused for a moment, and then continued. "But there is one thing I really wish they would do around here."

"What's that?" I asked.

"They really need signs for the tourists."

"What do you mean?"

"For example," she said, "there are these big things out in the fields spraying out water or something. They need signs to tell us what that is all about."

"Those are sprinklers," I replied. "And they water the crops."

"Why do they need to water the crops?" she asked.

"You know how you said that, where you are from, it rains sometimes twice per day? Well, here, it rains sometimes twice per summer, so we have to water everything or it will die."

This really stunned her. She thought about it a moment, and then asked, "And what is that tall golden and green grass in the fields?"

"That is wheat," I told her. "It is mostly ripe, and that is why it is mostly golden. The part that is not ripe is still green, but it will all be golden in a couple of weeks."

"And what about the fields of dark green stuff that is about two feet high?"

"Those are potatoes," I answered.

She grinned at that. "I have always wanted to know what potatoes look like, and to think that I have seen fields and fields of them and didn't even know that's what they were."

"Is there anything else you want to know about?" I asked.

"There is one more thing," she replied. "I see miles and miles of this grey, woody bush. What is that?"

I had to think a minute to figure out what that one was, but I suddenly realized what she was talking about. "Oh, that is sagebrush."

"What do they grow it for, western movie sets?"

I smiled, but shook my head. "No, it grows naturally. No one grows it; it just grows on wild land that no one plants with another crop."

We visited for a little while longer, and then, when I went home, I told Donna about my conversation with the woman. "Can you believe that someone doesn't know what potatoes look like?" I asked, laughing. "I guess we do need to start putting up signs for the tourists."

She smiled at me. "Don't think it is too unusual. When I first moved here from Los Angeles, I felt the same way that woman does."

Soon we headed on our vacation. As we traveled along the Pacific Coast Highway, certain plants intrigued me. "Honey, what do you think these fields of bluish green plants are?" I asked.

Donna just smiled. "I don't know, Dear. Maybe they need to put up some signs for the tourists."

What Bravery Isn't

I wasn't very popular in 3rd grade, so when a group of boys allowed me to be part of their group, I was very excited. I realize that it was likely because I wasn't the best marble player and they knew they could win against me, but I was happy to have any acceptance at all.

That was why the day they were picking on Tia was so hard for me. Tia had just moved to our school and, though she was very nice, she was also extremely shy. Her clothes were neat and clean, but they were worn and out of style, indicating that her family had little money. I was just heading out to recess when I ran into my friends in the hall. Tia was there. The boys were teasing her, her books were scattered on the floor, and she had tears in her eyes.

"Wow, aren't you a clumsy one?" one boy said to her.

"What would you expect from a book worm?" another said.

I stood there, frozen for a moment, my young mind whirling. If I helped her I knew they would tease me, and they might not want me in their group anymore. But as I continued to watch, I finally could stand it no longer, for I had endured the same thing too many times. I stepped between her and the boys and faced my friends. "Leave her alone," I said.

My voice quivered slightly, though I tried to act brave. Not only was this likely to destroy what little social standing I had, but some of the boys were as much as three years older than I was.

The boys seemed surprised, but then one of the biggest ones laughed. "Hey guys," he said, "it looks like Buzz Cut has a girl friend."

Hearing one of my former, hated nicknames, I took a deep breath. But, still, I held my ground. They teased me and laughed some more, then one said, "Come on guys. Let's go play and leave Buzz Cut with his sweetheart."

One of the bigger boys punched me really hard in my

shoulder as they turned to leave. "Have fun," he said, "and don't come playing with us. We don't want no sissies."

Once they were gone, I turned to Tia. "Are you all right?" I asked. She just nodded. I helped her pick up her books and then she quickly left, not saying a word.

I stood there, feeling very much alone, when the janitor, Mr. Bandon, stepped out of the shadows. I hadn't realized that he had watched the whole thing. "That was a very brave thing to do," he said.

"It wasn't brave," I replied. "I was scared to death."

He stopped right in front of me and spoke kindly. "Bravery is not a lack of fear, but the courage to do what is right, in spite of that fear."

"But they were all my friends," I said. "My teacher, Mrs. Moeller, said that bravery is the courage to stand up to your enemies."

He smiled kindly. "That may be true, and it is definitely part of it, but it is not all." He put his hand on my shoulder. "Perhaps you need to come with me." He led me down to his office, if that's what it could be called. It was full of brooms, mops, and cleaning supplies, but it did have a desk. On one wall were some pictures. It was in front of these that we stopped.

He motioned to one with a large group of men dressed in military uniforms. "You might not know that I served in World War II," he said. He then pointed to one man. "I admire this man more than any of the others, and do you know why?" I shook my head, so he continued. "The courage to stand up to the enemy was pretty much forced upon us, and he was as strong in that way as anyone. But what set him apart was that he would stand up for the right, even against those who were supposed to be his friends."

"You see," he said, turning to look at me, "sometimes it takes more courage to stand up to one's friends than it does to stand up to one's enemies."

Courage To Stand Up To Friends

When I stood up to my friends, defending a new girl at my school, the janitor, Mr. Bandon, saw the whole thing. He told me that it can take more courage to stand up to friends than to enemies. That was when he showed me a picture in his office of men from his World War II battalion, and shared the story of Private Johnson, the man he said he admired most.

Their battalion had fought across Europe, incurring heavy losses in the Battle Of The Bulge. As the Germans ran out of supplies and started to retreat, the Americans set up a base camp. The supply trucks hadn't yet come, and what food they had was moldy and stale. They threw away the worst, and ate what they could.

Most of the local Germans were starving, having what little food they owned taken from them for the army. That night, some of them snuck into the camp to take the rotten food that had been thrown away, but they were captured. The next day, the commanding Colonel, still angry at the losses his battalion had suffered, ordered the Germans to be shot.

Mr. Bandon and Private Johnson were among those chosen for the firing squad. The Germans were brought out. They had suffered great deprivation, and most of them were so thin that their flesh hung loosely over their bodies. They were all just boys and old men, because the fighting age men had been taken for war. The Germans were lined up, frightened and begging for their lives, but the Colonel felt little mercy.

He gave the orders. "Ready! Aim!"

That was when Private Johnson lowered his rifle and spoke. "Sir, I can't shoot them."

The Colonel was furious at this insubordination. He had Private Johnson step forward. "You will do as you are told," the Colonel ordered.

Private Johnson shook his head. "I can't. It isn't right. They are starving and just trying to find food for their families. They took nothing except what we threw away."

The Colonel stood there, seething in his anger. When he finally spoke, he nearly spit out his words. "They are the enemy. If you can't do your job, then you can take their place. You have a choice. Either do as you are commanded, or release them and be shot yourself. Now, get back in line!"

But Private Johnson didn't get back in line. He walked to the Germans while everyone stared after him. He pulled his knife, and the German prisoners trembled. But he didn't hurt them. Instead, he cut the ropes that held them. He then motioned for them to go. They stood for a moment until he motioned to them again, then they ran off as fast as they could.

Then he did something no one there would ever forget. He stepped to the wall where the Germans had stood, bowed his head in prayer for a moment, then looked up and said, "I'm ready."

He closed his eyes and waited. The Colonel had not expected this, and his subdued voice quivered with emotion. "Ready." Some of the men raised their guns to the ready, but most refused, Mr. Bandon being one of them. "Aim," came the next command. Private Johnson closed his eyes to wait. He started to tremble from fear, but ready to die, rather than kill innocent people. Mr. Bandon closed his eyes, unable to watch.

But no order came. When Mr. Bandon finally opened his eyes, the Colonel had stepped in front of the guns. He had an expression on his face that showed the emotion he felt at the display of courage Private Johnson had shown. The Colonel motioned for the men to lower their rifles, and then he turned to Private Johnson.

"Johnson," the Colonel bellowed, "you have a new assignment."

"Sir?" Private Johnson questioned.

"You choose yourself a few men to help you, and you make sure that any food we are disposing of is distributed to anyone who can use it. That is an order. Do you understand?"

Private Johnson smiled. "Yes, Sir."

Mr. Bandon joined Private Johnson in this endeavor, and they became good friends.

"So, you see," Mr. Bandon told me, "sometimes it can take even more courage to stand up to friends than it does to enemies."

The Greatest Courage Of All

I was only in third grade when our school janitor, Mr. Bandon, felt I had done something courageous, and shared with me some stories of courage about an army buddy of his named Private Johnson. He told me how Private Johnson had courageously stood up to his own friends, even when it was tough. "But there was one other time he showed great courage," Mr. Bandon said. He then told me one more story.

The Germans were gradually retreating as the Allied forces were fighting their way across Europe. Now and then the Germans would make a stand, but they were losing their will to fight and would soon continue their retreat.

At one point, Mr. Bandon's battalion came to the edge of a potato field that was about two hundred yards across. It was late fall, and the ground was frozen and the air was cold. A German battalion ended up reaching the opposite side of the open field at about the same time, and both sides opened fire, both with rifles and heavy artillery.

Two young girls, unaware of the two approaching armies, had been out in the potato field trying to dig through the hard soil for anything they could find to eat. When the firing started, they dropped to the ground, frightened and crying. After the shooting had gone on for a short time, without any warning, Private Johnson suddenly ran out from behind the heavy armaments and ran toward the girls in the midst of a hailstorm of bullets.

The firing gradually subsided as both sides curiously watched to see what he was up to. He ran to the two frightened girls and tucked one under each arm.

Everyone expected him to turn and run back to the safety of his own line, but he didn't. Looking up and seeing a small home at the edge of the enemy position, he saw the frightened mother screaming for her daughters. He ran toward the home, right into the line of the enemy.

German soldiers were there with the mother to meet him, and he handed the girls to them. The crying mother fell on her knees at his feet and scooped the two little girls into her arms, sobbing her gratitude.

Private Johnson then turned and ran back to his line, while both sides still held their fire. Even after he crossed back to the American position, and collapsed from loss of blood, no one fired. Both sides seemed unable to fight after seeing this selfless act of kindness performed by a soldier in behalf of daughters of his enemy. The German battalion just moved on in their retreat, and the American battalion held their position and did not pursue them.

Mr. Bandon knelt down beside his wounded friend and worked with others trying to stem the flow of blood. The battalion colonel, who had once almost had Private Johnson shot for standing up to him against an order that was wrong, came up beside them.

He looked down at Private Johnson and shook his head. "Johnson, you are a fool!" He then paused, as the tears started flowing down his war hardened face, the only time Mr. Bandon ever saw him cry. "You are a fool, Johnson, but I wish I was half the man you are."

Private Johnson looked up, smiled, and then closed his eyes, never to open them again. He had given his life for children of the enemy.

Mr. Bandon finished his story. "Somewhere in Europe stands a marker. Whether it even has a name on it, I don't know. But it represents the life of the most courageous man I have ever known. He showed courage to do what was right in every situation he faced, and finally, in the end, he did so in one of the greatest challenges of all." He paused briefly, trying to control his emotions, then finally continued.

"The rest of us bravely stood up to the enemy, but if it was right, he courageously stood up **for** the enemy, and that takes the most courage of all."

If you enjoyed our book, we would love to have you do a review on Amazon at:
http://amzn.com/162986000X

Would you like to see Life's Outtakes column running in your local paper or magazine? Suggest it to the editor. If an editor runs the Life's Outtakes column due to your suggestion, we will send you one of Daris Howard's books, of your choice, signed by the author. Find out more at:

http://www.darishoward.com

Read other stories, purchase more books, or sign up for a short story each week by going to

http://www.darishoward.com

Other books
by
Daris Howard
Daris Howard Amazon page:
http://amzn.com/e/B004H76UGK

 **When The World Goes Crazy**
Life's Outtakes Year 1
http://amzn.com/B004O0U8ZO

 **All's Well Here**
Life's Outtakes Year 2
http://amzn.com/B007AQB5TW

 **When Life Is More Than We Dreamed**
Life's Outtakes Year 3
http://amzn.com/B007DNL286

 **Nothing But A Miracle**
Life's Outtakes Year 4
http://amzn.com/B0087FZE56

	**Singing To The End Of Life** **Life's Outtakes Year 5** http://amzn.com/B0087FB9G4
	**It's Ninety Percent Mental** **Life's Outtakes Year 6** http://amzn.com/B00AYRTS48

Other Books

Under Open Skies - **Born To Run, Live To Be Free** http://amzn.com/1629860042

In this second book in the *Under Open Skies* series, Tom Johnson is now 25 years old and married. Going to school and trying to take care of his family, he gets a job taking care of horses. When the lady he works for purchases an old, former race horse, and Tom needs to take care of him, Tom learns the true meaning of freedom.

Super Cowboy Rides - http://amzn.com/1937178021 Meet six-year-old Tommy Johnson, Super Cowboy and Super Story-teller. When Tommy explains why a boy needs a dog for a pet instead of a cat, he wins everyone over with his down-to-earth and humorous view of the world. But once Tommy starts school, things get complicated.

One reviewer wrote: "The little boy, Tommy, reminds me of Calvin from the "Calvin and Hobbs" comic strip. It is such a fun book to read!" - **Celese Sanders** (syndicated columnist of "Little Bits Of Life")

Essence Of The Heart, The Royal Tutor -
http://amzn.com/1479392189

Mystery, Intrigue, And Clean Romance!

When he is called before the queen, Jacob, the handsome, young Captain of the Royal Guard, is sure it is to discuss the baffling increase in assassination attempts against the royal family. Instead, the queen assigns the shocked young captain to tutor her out-of-control, tomboy daughter, Marie.

Angry and humiliated at what he feels is a degrading and impossible assignment, especially for a military captain, he determines to train the princess like he would one of his guardsmen. He will demand strong discipline, tough academics, and sword combat training. He is sure that his rigorous approach will push the princess to complain to her mother, who will then remove him from the assignment.

But to his surprise, Marie instead responds positively to the harsh discipline, and becomes a princess like no other.

And, when they come under attack, her training might be just enough to save both of their lives as they work to unravel who is behind the assassination attempts, and also try to solve the mystery of why the Lord High Chamberlain is such a great sword fighter.

The Mail-Order Bride -
http://amzn.com/1480200387

It was to be the big day for Eli. His fiancée, Molly, was coming in on a ship. Two years earlier, unable to find work in England, he had headed for America. His ship was caught in a storm, and he ended up, not in Pennsylvania as he planned, but in Newfoundland.

But that was all behind him now. He had written to Molly every day for the two years, and now she was coming so they could be married.

But Eli was in for a surprise. Unknown to him, Molly had married. She had bought him a mail-order bride, and Eli's life was going to suddenly take an unexpected twist.

The Three Gifts - http://amzn.com/1449961436

A beautiful Christmas story about three young men who are convicted of mugging little children for their Halloween candy. Instead of sentencing them to jail, as is expected, the judge sentences them to 100 hours of community service babysitting at the Women's Crisis Center.

They were prepared for jail, but they were not prepared for what was in store for them as the children opened their eyes and hearts and changed their lives.

For inspiring plays and books, as well as discounts for book sellers, go to

http://www.publishinginspiration.com

About The Author

Daris Howard is an author and playwright who grew up on a farm in rural Idaho. He associated with many colorful characters including cowboys, farmers, lumberjacks and others. Besides his work on the farm he has worked as a cowboy and a mechanic. He was a state champion athlete and competed in college athletics. He also lived for eighteen months in New York.

Daris and his wife, Donna, have ten children and were foster parents for several years. He has also worked in scouting and cub scouts, at one time having 18 boys in his scout troop.

His plays, musicals, and books build on the characters of those he has associated with, along with his many experiences, to bring his work to life.

Daris is a math professor and his classes are well known for the stories he tells to liven up discussion and to help bring across the points he is trying to teach. His scripts and books are much like his stories, full of humor and inspiration.

He and his family have enjoyed running a summer community theatre where he gets a chance to premiere his theatrical works and rework them to make them better. His published plays and books can be seen at http://www.darishoward.com. He has plays translated into German and French and his work has been done in many countries around the world.

In the last few years, Daris has started writing books and short stories. He writes a popular news column called *Life's Outtakes*, that consists of weekly short stories and is published in various newspapers and magazines in the U.S. and Canada including **Country**, **Horizons**, and **Family Living**.

www.ingramcontent.com/pod-product-compliance
Lightning Source LLC
Chambersburg PA
CBHW060629130626
46555CB00002B/721